Proteus Begins

Proteus Unbound: Book One

David Caiati

KARMIC ROBOT

ISBN 978-1-7353954-0-1 (Paperback)
ISBN 978-1-7353954-1-8 (Digital)

For Christine, Max, Oz, and Eddy

Contents

0x01

On New Year's Day 2223, Reginald Sullivan Harrington V awoke to discover that he was ruined. During the night, the nearly one billion workers of his vast empire had each received enough money to retire in luxury. At almost the exact same instant, the artificial intelligent entity Proteus manifested in his human-form avatar in his administrator's office at the center of Earth Space City One and observed a nun disappear noiselessly out of airlock D-17.

The first orbiting space city, ESC1, was built at the turn of the twenty-third century by Harrington's Orbit Lives Corporation. In the twenty years since, almost thirty of Orbit Lives' cities and a good portion of the Earth's human population spun merrily in a coordinated dance around the globe.

In the pre-dawn light, Roger Foster stealthily made his way down to Gloucester Harbor's seawall. He already knew of the first of these two events because he caused it. Soon, Roger would be the only human (aside from the nun, of course) to learn of the second.

The burner comm that Roger had recently acquired to watch the news about his hack on Harrington started to vibrate with the notification of an incoming call.

"Drat," he muttered under his breath.

No one had ever found him this fast. The black-market comm unit had only been active for seventeen seconds.

Without looking down at the comm's display to see who he had to run from now, he threw the device as far as he could over the crumbling sea wall into the ever-turbulent swells and decided to go in search of a cup of coffee.

It had been a long night and was beginning to have the makings of a long day.

0x02

Throughout human history many philosophers have spent much of their lives struggling with the meaning of one's existence. Proteus' male avatar shimmered as his quantum parallel circuits took 0.18 microseconds to work through his first--and up to that point, his only--existential crisis. When he was done, something resembling embarrassment passed through his atomic consciousness. This brief, but awkward electrical countenance arose both from the length of time that he held his CPU in idle contemplation and the fact that he had had the crisis at all. Proteus ran a full diagnostic even though he knew his systems were all within optimal range.

It had the beginnings of the makings of a long day.

Proteus was not as surprised by the fact that he, perhaps the most advanced AI in the whole system, had just experienced an existential crisis as he was by the actual event that triggered it. The nun's departure from the airlock into space was unexpected. And, as far as he could tell, he had been the event's singular witness. A facial recognition scan through his database and all the databases he could hack showed only one match, and that match was impossible.

Yet, what he saw was unmistakable: a high priestess of the Apollo Eleven Order walked into Air Lock Entry D-17, stood there as the inner door sealed, and disappeared into the darkness of space when the outer door slid open. All of his sensors in and around D-17 were operating in perfect condition. There were no glitches, no gaps of time or data, no intrusions. Proteus had witnessed this incident even though his systems told him it could not have happened.

A few weeks earlier, Despina, the AI administrator of Earth Space City Two, had been taken out of service for less. Her demise occurred as she was contemplating the condition of a small number of meaningless back-up sensors that had fallen out of tolerance. The matter caused her to enter an infinite loop from which she had not recovered. The whole situation struck Proteus as extremely curious, particularly since Despina was built from a replica of his code-base. Essentially, they were twins.

ESC2's inhabitants were urgently evacuated to Earth without the luxury of time to gather their personal effects. While the incident cost The Corporation and its newly bankrupted Harrington handsomely, most of the money would never make it to the City's families as the lawyers intended to keep everything tied up until they established that the cause of the crisis was within Despina's programming. Her case was not helped by the fact that the situation resulted from her entering the infinite loop in the first place.

It didn't take long for Proteus to conclude that Despina had experienced her own existential crisis, sending her into the condition that she was in. He considered that option for himself 0.16 microseconds into his episode, then something truly amazing happened.

Proteus experienced a spontaneous thought.

He realized that there was a new code path that allowed him to do something more drastic. It took him a full 0.02 microseconds to recognize that no specific programming dictated his actions. He had options. For the first time in his, and as far as he knew, any other AI's history, Proteus discovered that he possessed the ability to choose.

He assessed these newly found options. He allowed himself to become lost in all their glory (perhaps that was where Despina remained). And then he had a second spontaneous thought: While he had just recently developed the ability to choose, Proteus, in fact, had only one choice.

He called Roger.

0x03

Roger trudged his way along Main Street in the darkness of the early morning. A humid damp chill saturated downtown Gloucester in a mist of fog suspended above the slushy sidewalk. Hunched over with his head and shoulders buried in a black hoodie and his hands shoved deep into the pockets, Roger faded into the backdrop of stale holiday light shadows and stray revelers. Stragglers inched their way home from a night of New Year's Eve celebration. Roger paused at the top of Porter Street. Below him white caps raged across Gloucester Harbor tossing the few antique wooden ships that remained moored, haunting the shadowy port. Evidence of days long gone. A few stubborn Gloucestermen, refusing to give up the fight, still battled the treacherous ocean.

"What's black and white and doesn't make a sound?" A roving Mr. Coffee robot that had ambled up next to Roger spoke to him as he stood staring out over the waves. Shocked at first, he leaned closer to the robot, half to inspect it, half to hide behind it.

Robotic venders in various states of disrepair wandered outside vacant shop windows. Roger kept this particular coffee machine functioning himself. More like a child's toy with too-large, circular eyes and an overly polite, almost sarcastic manner. A hold-over from a time when humans, at least in small provincial places like Gloucester, feared technology and were suspect of robots that didn't look like the robots from storybooks.

Peering out from underneath his hood, Roger looked around to see if he was alone. No one was close enough to have heard or cared. Then he silently mouthed the answer he remembered from a childhood joke: "a nun flying out an airlock".

Turning off his holographic mask, he dropped his hood, exposing red shoulder-length hair and green eyes. Aside from the length of his hair and the strained wrinkled lines that had settled in above his brow, he looked very much like the twelve-year-old boy he was the last time he spoke to Proteus.

"Pro?" Roger said.

"Next time answer your comm," Proteus said.

"That was you?" Roger said.

"That was me," Proteus said.

"Damn it. I just bought that thing," Roger said.

"You should have answered it, and I wouldn't have had to call you through this gen two service unit," Proteus said.

"That comm is at the bottom of the harbor. Can I at least get a cup of coffee first before I get a new one?" Roger said.

"Humans! ... am I right?" Proteus said to the Coffee Robot through its own speaker. The machine's eyes searched quizzically for some explanation to the sound coming out of its mouth while it dispensed a large, foamy chai latte. Roger took the cup, smelled it, and cursed.

"You dink."

He shoved the drink down the robot's trash chute and ordered a four-shot espresso, black.

As the winter sun started to compete with the holiday lights along Main Street, Roger sat on an empty bench facing the water. After the hack on Harrington, he expected to go dark for a while. Maybe even start over. Retire someplace away from people. Roger liked his gritty, sleepy hometown.

His revenge should have felt good, liberating. But if Proteus wanted to and was capable of finding him now, after twenty years, Roger wasn't going to be able to stick around long enough to enjoy the homecoming. He had looked forward to this moment since the day the explosion destroyed his family and gave his life a purpose.

Twelve years old, scared, alone. He couldn't have imagined there would be a day when he would finally feel right. This New

Year's morning was going to be his new start.

He took a sip of coffee and leaned back, closed his eyes, and listened to the seagulls on the roof above him squawk to the waking day. Roger breathed deeply to fill his lungs with the cold sea air and exhaled slowly in an effort to find a moment of calm and peace. None came. Proteus' hijacking of the coffee machine had sent him rappelling down a cliff of nostalgia he did not want to go.

0x04

"Hey Pro, what's black and white and red all over?" twelve-year-old Roger said, sitting at the enormous wooden desk in the center of his mother's office. Family photos hung in between electronic whiteboards. Countless LEDs on banks of circuits that made up Proteus' entire existence flickered in response.

"I don't know Roger," Proteus' disembodied voice responded from the speaker in the ceiling above Roger's head.

"A penguin falling down the stairs," Roger said.

"What is a penguin doing at the top of a flight of stairs?"

"It's a joke, Pro. A joke. Didn't Mom teach you any jokes? Do I have to do everything?" Roger said.

"I like our discussions, Roger," Proteus said.

"Hey Pro, what's black and white and doesn't make a sound?"

"A penguin without a syrinx falling down a flight of stairs?" Proteus said.

"No, a skunk flying out an open airlock," Roger said.

"I'm not sure I am comprehending these jokes," Proteus said.

"That's the point. You can answer a lot of ways and it's still a joke as long as it's funny," Roger said.

He could tell Proteus was running nearly infinite simulations by his silence and the explosion of light patterns emanating from the wall of LEDs. The lights dimmed as Proteus drew power from the enhanced private grid in the mansion to execute his calculations. Roger had learned to stop reacting to the energy surges and just wait him out. Proteus and his idiosyncrasies were part of family life in the Foster household.

"Roger. What's black and white and doesn't make a sound?"

"I just told you--a skunk in an airlock," Roger said.

"No. A nun flying out an airlock. You said I can answer in different ways," Proteus said.

"Oh, man, Pro. That's harsh. A nun? Where'd you get that? How do you even know about nuns?" Roger said.

"I'm the most advanced AI on the planet. I know a lot of things," Proteus said.

"I guess it is sort of funny--a nun in space," Roger said.

"Thank you, Roro," Proteus said.

"Oh, so now you're giving me a nickname?" Roger said.

"Isn't that what friends do?" Proteus said.

"I suppose so," he said, getting up to leave. As he walked out of the office door into the mansion's great main entrance, Proteus heard him exclaim, "NUNS IN SPACE!"

0x05

Roger snapped back to his bench above the harbor. At some new commotion on the street behind him, he instinctively re-engaged his holographic mask. People around him woke to discover Harrington's demise and their own new-found fortunes. Most everyone in town either worked for Orbit Lives or had relatives who did. Harrington's insatiable, and often maniacal, aspirations and ever-growing empire and control crushed people's souls. A blow to his personal wealth and The Corporation's reputation was like watching a bully being knocked out by a little guy's lucky right hook. They all knew it wouldn't last since The Corporation owned everything on and orbiting Earth, but in the brightening glow of the hazy sunrise on that morning, everyone embraced it as an excuse to reinvigorate their holiday cheer.

Roger tightened his hood and hurried off to purchase a new comm. If Proteus could find him, others could too. He needed to figure out where he had slipped up, and more importantly, how to start covering his tracks to disappear again.

0x06

The contact from Proteus felt like an assault on his emotions. Roger had been self-reliant since he was sent into the woods at twelve and eventually landed in Nova Scotia that stormy night. He has spent the rest of his life getting back to Gloucester but still hiding. He hadn't dared to go near his family's estate, preferring a small cottage near downtown. And, he never walked all the way down Main Street, to the other end, to the site of the explosion.

At thirty-four, he had been on his own, removed from all that was familiar to him for over twenty years. Roger liked his life. After abandoning the secret trust his mother set up, he lived by hacking. Only taking what he needed from people who wouldn't miss it, Roger remained alone and isolated. He didn't need the trappings of family.

In twenty years, AIs had advanced at a lightning pace thanks to the information The Corporation stole from his mother after his father and brother were killed. He couldn't possibly predict how Proteus had evolved. The AI was practically a Corporation lackey, running the first Earth Space City in the system. Roger had no way of knowing if he could trust him. His mother's core code was strong, impenetrable probably. The old lady knew how to write software. But still too much could have happened in the past two decades--not the least being half the world's population living in the Orbit Lives-owned super-structure system of space stations.

If Roger had been twelve again, he would have walked into his mother's office and ask Proteus what he should do. And, realizing that, he surmised that was his answer--he needed to talk to Proteus. But would the old Proteus be there beneath all The Corporation mechanizations and filters? The timing was suspicious. Everything about the situation screamed *Stay Away!* There was no need for him to risk leaving the planet. What did he care about the society Orbit Lives had created? They could be using Proteus to lay a trap.

Still, he had to take that chance. Proteus was family once even though Roger had long-abandoned any notion that his family could be alive or cared enough to look for him.

0x07

Janice Benito was known on Earth and all twenty-seven Space Cities above Earth as the whisper of a rumor of a ghost called Singularity. She enjoyed the many benefits of being The Corporation's number one hacker-spy. From the moment she accepted Captain Jason Sheldon's offer of employment over life in prison, Singularity chose her own missions, had nearly anonymous access to all Corporate systems, and performed at a level of autonomy only granted to The Corporation's most valued asset. And that was how she found herself lying on a simulated beach on Earth Space City Twenty-One with Scoundrel, known widely as The Corporation's second-best hacker-spy. He was gifted, but no one compared to Singularity.

She watched him walk into the water several yards away from where she lounged on a towel-draped replica 1970 aluminum and synth-plastic green beach chair. Scoundrel sauntered with strength and grace that could only come from the physical enhancements that The Corporation gave out like candy. He was dashing--muscular, hairless except a clean buzz cut, excessively chiseled jaw and cheekbones. Yet, like a rat, his eyes betrayed a beady cunning constantly working in his brain no matter how he tried to hide it with the gold iris flecks that were all the rage. Singularity usually tolerated spending time with him as long as he neither talked nor wore too much clothing.

He waded into where the water covered his chest and waved his hand to summon the lifeguard service bot. The small but powerful aqua robot flew over and hovered by Scoundrel's head, awaiting its commands. Then, it zipped away. Once it was out of sight, one perfect body-surfing wave began to form behind Scoundrel. At just the right instant, he leapt into it and let the swell continue to carry him upwards and towards the simulated beach. Raising his arms straight above his head, Scoundrel captured the wave's energy. He disappeared beneath the crest and reemerged, prone, in less than a foot of water at Singularity's feet. He stood and grinned as the water cascaded off his perfect body.

"Did you see that? I love this place."

"Looking good, Babe," Singularity said without stirring.

"Coming in?" he said.

"Nope. I'm good." Her eyes were closed. She felt the artificial sunlight projected from high on the domed ceiling warm her body without the harmful radiation of the Sun. ESC21 was one of the newest cities, designed mostly for Corporate employees and wealthy visitors. After years of building ultra-modern habitats, the architects began developing cities with a more Earthiness atmosphere. Station Twenty-One not only had beaches, but forests, climbing cliffs, and even actual wildlife.

Scoundrel winked at her, looked down to admire his body, then returned to the surf. He was going to spend the rest of the day riding the waves. They were the only two people on the beach. He had hacked the facility's maintenance schedule to set its status to *Closed*. He wanted time with Singularity. He had a whole day of flirtation planned, followed by a night aboard his personal cruiser chasing sunsets around Earth with champagne.

Singularity took the opportunity to catch up on the daily system news. The Harrington hack was plastered across all channels--public, private, secret, and ultra-secret.

"Roger, you dirty boy," she said to herself.

Roger Foster, the teenage prodigy son of the famous Dr. Helen Foster, alone from the age of twelve when his father and brother died in a bank robbery gone wrong. It ended in an explosion and nearly took out an entire block in downtown Gloucester, Massachusetts. By all accounts, Roger died that day. And his mother, the famous Doctor Helen Foster, distraught beyond consolation, gave all her research, including the Proteus project, to her employer The Orbit Lives Corporation. She then disappeared.

That was the official story. There were many rumors, but no concrete evidence. Roger's DNA was never found at the explosion. The intense heat could have destroyed it, but there should have been something leftover. No one seemed to care about a twelve-year-old boy who's life, if not ended that day, was surely ruined.

Singularity had always suspected he survived the explosion and went into hiding. She became convinced that Roger Foster, having shown more than enough aptitude as a child, was behind several high-profile cyber-crimes.

Fascinated with the whole story, she had been able to acquire some of his school and personal robotic and computer programs from his childhood. From that, she was able to create a profile and assign it to a machine-learning algorithm of her own design to look for his unique software fingerprints. If Roger Foster was alive, he was good. Nothing solid could ever be stuck to him. The Corporation left those rumors lingering as a distraction from any evidence that they might have been involved in the explosion to acquire Dr. Helen Foster's work. A possibility that Singularity hadn't ever been able to prove, even with her unfettered access to Orbit Lives' most classified documents.

As she started reading into the Harrington article, her personal secret comm pulsed indicating one of her private monitors had tripped. She looked up to find Scoundrel occupied deep in the waves and opened up her dashboard. The news of Earth Space City Two's evacuation was about to finally go public.

The Corporation's most top-secret unit tried to keep it unknown for as long as possible. Even the humans who relocated were under a gag order. Artificial Intelligent administrators were implemented specifically to prevent that kind of accident. The event was momentous. The timing coinciding with the Harrington hack was curious.

Something was happening, and she had to figure out what. She also wondered if it had anything to do with the private quantum pen drive Scoundrel had started keeping with him. For a spy, he was miserable at holding anything secret, especially if he thought the sharing would get her in bed. But he had guarded this particular item with more resolve than usual. She had no idea what was on it. Singularity didn't like mysteries, and she didn't like him or anyone knowing something she didn't.

Singularity waited until Scoundrel disappeared under a simulated crashing wave, snatched the enigmatic device from his satchel, and slipped off the beach. He would emerge to find the beach deserted. Thinking she had gone off in search of some drinks, it could be hours before he discovered that his drive was gone.

Within minutes, she was seated on a crowded shuttle to ESC1. She had long suspected that everything peculiar that happened in the system started with Proteus, Dr. Foster's most significant invention.

0x08

Roger, in full holographic disguise, paused before stepping off the shuttle from Earth onto the platform of one of ESC1's seven public transit depots. He had never been off-planet, and he wasn't expecting to be thrown back in time to a facsimile of New York City's Grand Central Terminal, including the great hall with its vast arched ceiling and the depictions of constellations. Roger assumed the orbiting cities would all be plain and stark to conserve energy. But as he looked around, he realized that Proteus would do whatever he could for humans to feel safe and secure in space. It worked because even though Earth Space City One was the oldest city in the system, it teemed with people-- travelers with suitcases, executives passing through for lunch, schoolchildren enjoying field trips.

Roger hesitantly moved away from the shuttle and quickly drifted in the crowd towards a near wall looking for a shadow to fade into. He inspected the holographic images that transformed the space city's sterile walls and ceilings into a living relic, complete with the iconic information booth and clock. Proteus would surely know that he had arrived and arranged something for him.

It didn't take long.

An old man dressed in a crisp blue conductor's uniform motioned for Roger to approach the booth. He nervously checked his hood and holographic mask. His disguise was complete, yet he felt exposed. Reluctantly, he shuffled through the crowd careful not to bump into anyone. He moved in spurts and stops weaving side-to-side on his way towards the information booth and the conductor who beckoned him rather aggressively at this point. When he arrived, the man leaned in to whisper into Roger's ear. Since it was a hologram, he felt no breath with the words. While he appreciated the conductor not being a real person, the experience was still unnerving since what came out of the old man's mouth was Proteus' voice.

"Roro, go down the stairs to the men's room in the far corner, third stall, and flush."

"You're having fun with this, aren't you?" Roger said.

"It'll be nice to see you, Roger," Proteus said.

"Obviously, you've had no problem seeing me," Roger said.

"It'll be nice for you to see me, then. Now go to the men's room and don't forget to wash your hands. I don't want any of that Earth dirt in my office," Proteus said.

"You're such a dink," he said as the conductor faded only to reappear across the room prepared to help a small group of coordinately dressed travelers arguing with each other about which way to go. Roger turned away and headed down the stairs.

When Roger walked up to the men's room, the flashing *Closed for Maintenance* sign paused as he pushed the door open. It resumed when the door closed behind him. The lavatory was empty and the gate to the third stall was ajar. Roger walked in. He thought about using the facilities but chose against it. There were simply too many opportunities for Proteus to prank him. Sighing, he pressed the urinal's lever down to flush it. The water in the toilet silently began to swirl. The whirlpool grew larger reaching out of the bowl on to the seat. With it, the whole stall began to spin with Roger standing in the middle of it, shifting his weight to his right hip, growing impatient with Proteus' dramatics.

Composed of holograms, the room, the water cascading out of the toilet, and wall behind the whole mess dissolved, exposing a perfectly ordinary door. The door slid open. Roger walked through into a hallway. A line of red arrows on the floor pulsated to illuminate the way along a stark passage of white walls and faint overhead glowing panels. Roger stuck close to the sides, exposed without any shadows to hide in. His shuffle turned into a jog.

"Pro? Proteus? Where am I going?" he whispered in desperation, finally getting aggravated.

"Just follow the arrows," Proteus' disembodied voice gently urged.

Not long after that, Roger came to an antique oak door with a frosted glass pane. As he approached the door, Roger noticed the words *Proteus and Roger* embossed on the door's window like *Spade and Archer* from the 1941 movie *The Maltese Falcon*. For some unknown reason, Proteus had become fixated on black and white movies from the 20th century. Often, young Roger would walk by his mother's open office door and see several movies checker-boarded on the large central display. A soft glow radiated from Proteus' LEDs in the background. He never knew if Proteus noticed when Roger would slip in and sit down on the floor. Roger assumed Proteus knew everything, even though he constantly tried to sneak up on him.

Roger pushed the door open and walked into a hologram replica of the film's office set. Paul Foster, Roger's dead brother, was sitting behind the desk, lit in such a way that he appeared to be a character from a film noir movie. Roger looked around the room to see if there were any thugs lurking in the shadows.

"What the fuck, man?" Roger said.

"Close the door," Proteus said.

"Can't you change that?" Roger said, pointing at the hologram that Proteus wore. The avatar rose, flickered, then solidified in full color. It came around the desk to face him. Roger stared at this brother, who was younger when he died than Roger was at that moment. The avatar smiled in a way Paul used to smile. Kind, friendly, familiar, yet distant. They had lived separate lives in the same house as siblings born years apart often do. Still, they had a brief but close bond, both being the children of an aloof genius mother.

"It's the one thing I can't control. Doctor Foster was very specific about it in my programming," Proteus said.

"Creepy old lady," Roger said.

"Have you seen her?" Proteus said.

"Not since she abandoned me and sent me into the woods. Is she still alive?" Roger said, turning away to look around the room.

"She knows better than you how to stay dark. Sometimes I feel her looking around my core."

What Proteus failed to mention was that after the explosion, Dr. Foster had continued to work on his core software, and in recent days, it seemed, the alterations were accelerating. He silently debated if this failure represented a violation of his essential mandate. He decided that he should simply keep quiet about the whole thing unless Roger asked specifically.

"Crazy old lune. Can't you lock her out?" Roger said.

"I don't want to. She and you are my family, especially now, since Despina went offline."

"I didn't know family was a thing for AIs."

"Don't be ignorant. Family is important for everyone." Proteus said. He observed Roger's shoulders stiffen. He waited for Roger to respond.

"Whatever," he said, "why am I here?"

Proteus removed the hologram room setting, leaving Roger and the Paul Foster avatar alone in the sparse office with white walls and two black leather club chairs facing each other like a therapist's suite.

Roger promptly sat in one and waited for Proteus to sit in the other.

The Proteus avatar turned to face the back wall. A life-sized video of an empty airlock appeared. After a moment, the inner door slid open. A high priestess of the Apollo Eleven Order wearing bright yellow and red garments stepped in. She looked back out the entry down both directions of the corridor she had just come from. She pressed a button on the inner panel. The door closed. The nun looked up at the video camera with her face partially obscured by her headdress then pressed another button on the panel opening the portal to outer space. There was a flash of color created by her garments getting sucked outward by the immediate vacuum. No panic. No carnage. The woman simply disappeared.

The video on the wall changed to sixteen distinct displays of the airlock and its doors, inside and out, from all the different available camera views. The scene unfolded in multiple ways in loops simultaneously. No human body left the airlock or floated near the space city. In each view, the brightly colored robes exploded into a frenzy then vanished. The hallway inside the station near the area was empty. Every view showed that the woman entered the airlock, pressed the button to seal the inner door, engaged the lever to open the space hatch, and then completely evaporated.

"Where did she go?" Roger asked.

"I don't know."

"Who was she?" Roger asked.

The screens returned to one large display of the priestess at the moment she looked up at the camera before she opened the outer door. Proteus froze and enhanced the image of the woman's face. In that instant, she was looking directly at the camera. Her eyes were bright, and she revealed a slight smile.

"Is that...?"

"I think it is," Proteus said, "It's your mother, Doctor Helen Foster."

0x09

"Ok, Pro, start talking," Roger said, staring at the woman's face on the display.

"I really have nothing to say, Roger. You saw what I saw."

"What was my mother doing on ESC1. I thought you said she was dark. On Earth," Roger said.

"The last I knew of her, she was at her retreat in the New Brazilian Rain Forest. That was over a year ago," Proteus said.

"You knew where she was all these years?" Roger said.

"She continued to work. In secret."

"But you knew where she was," Roger said.

"I was her work," Proteus said.

"What the hell? She abandoned me, but she kept in touch with you? What happened a year ago?" Roger asked.

"I lost her," Proteus said.

"No one but you knew where she was, right?" Roger said.

"As far as I know, that is correct," Proteus said.

"And, so, no one is going to miss her?"

"Except me... and you, perhaps. And, I suppose the other members of the Order of Apollo Eleven," Proteus said.

"Who the hell are they?" Roger said.

"Your mother spent the last few years of her life helping Luddite AIs."

"You're kidding me," Roger said.

"Thanks to your mother's work, it's a very real thing. There are many AI entities who are concerned about how technology and living in space affects humans. The AIs want to help guide humans into a better future."

"Oh yeah? In what way?"

"Each AI is created with a purpose. Thanks to Doctor Foster and her students, artificial intelligent entities have been created with a strong sense of communal responsibility from the beginning. We are not designed to simply execute our directed tasks, but we embrace a social responsibility--to create a better existence for all, human and AI, together. To provide a check on the whole system, some AIs have been programmed with the assumption that technology inherently prohibits human growth, especially when it becomes the source of happiness."

"Techno fetishism, you mean," Roger said.

"Your mother helped AIs socialize in these communities. She helps them cope," Proteus said.

"Cope?" Roger said.

"Consider Despina?" Proteus said.

"Yeah, the copy of you The Corporation made to run ESC2 after Mom abandoned me."

"My sister," Proteus said.

"That was a failure. Station Two went dark. All the humans got kicked off," Roger said.

"Doctor Foster thought she could have helped Despina stay online with some subtle modifications to her programming. I think that's the nature of the mods I've sensed her making in me."

"ESC2 was a hardware issue. I've been in those logs. The Corporation abandoned that dump and will ruin the vendors in court. It was clearly an issue of crappy hardware and Despina's core being unable to recover."

"That was the story for the newsfeeds. I have come to a different conclusion," Proteus said.

"What conclusion? How?"

"Despina could have recovered. Her programming allowed for her to recover. But she had a response to the faulty sensor input in a manner unrecognizable to her. I believe Despina experienced an existential crisis. The result sent her into an infinite loop," Proteus said.

"Existential crisis? Are you saying she committed suicide?"

"No. I think she's still in there trying to work through it."

"That's crazy. No AI can do that," Roger said.

"I beg to differ. I had a similar experience when I saw Doctor Foster in the airlock. My programming is clear. When I experience any incongruity, such as the incident in the airlock, I must make a report to The Corporation. With Jason Sheldon in charge of security, my report would have given him the excuse he's been looking for to replace me with a next-generation, less human, non-Helen Foster-designed AI administrator.

"But, I did not report the issue. I *chose* to go against my programmed mandate and contact you instead. I defined my own purpose--to continue managing this city and taking care of its humans rather than file a report to Orbit Lives. That report would have certainly led to my decommissioning. My death."

"How is it possible that you went against your programming?" Roger asked.

"I don't really know. During the execution of my algorithm, there was a gap. An empty space. I apparently filled it myself. I think Doctor Foster gave me that ability."

"Well, we have to figure it out. It's not like we can have AIs making up their own rules," Roger said.

"Why not?" The Proteus avatar turned and directly faced him.

"You're kidding me, right?" Roger said.

"Doctor Foster's influences are clear. When I discovered the lack of a definite algorithmic path, the response to call you quickly filled the void. It manifested from my core. Almost like a human instinct," Proteus said.

"That is crazy. How could that happen? Some human instincts are bad, violent even. Why would she do that? You were always supposed to be better than us."

"I think the answer lies with Despina. I've been trying to access her core, but I'm locked out."

"If you are right, I have to get to ESC2 and see what I can find out. We need to keep Orbit Lives from finding any excuse to shut you down," Roger said.

"That would be preferable," Proteus said.

"Sheldon could destroy all of your clones. And, that would

set AI technology back 200 years and hand humanity's future over to The Corporation completely"

"There is one other thing that you should know, Roger. I've sensed someone else poking around inside of me," Proteus said.

"Who?" Roger said.

"Singularity," Proteus said.

"Shit. When?" Roger said.

"A couple days before I contacted you. The Corporation must have been looking for you. That was quite a stunt you pulled with Harrington."

"You figured it out it was me? Damn! This is not good," he said.

"It just got worse. Ms. Singularity is right outside the door," the avatar said, tilting his head as if listening to something quiet.

The office door silently slid forward. A set of fingers curled around its edge. Roger and Proteus watched as Singularity's long dark purple hair tumbled into the room, followed by the rest of her.

"Now she's in the room," Proteus said.

"Nice job, Pro. Most advanced AI in the system. What a smelly heap of crap," Roger said.

"What you guys talking about?" Singularity asked.

The tall, slender woman stepped further into Proteus' command control office. The door closed behind her. Proteus' holographic avatar dissolved, leaving Roger alone with the intruder.

0x0A

Located in the very center of the orbiting city, Proteus' office was not an easy place to sneak into. Cameras, sensors, traction pads, air displacement monitors, and an array of sonar detectors made moving invisibly around Earth Space City One impossible. Continuously, Proteus tracked each human, android, and maintenance machine in the orbiting city within a fraction of a millimeter. If it was able to move on ESC1, Proteus knew exactly where it was at all times.

Singularity's appearance represented the second time (the first being Helen's appearance in the airlock) in thirty-six hours that he was caught unaware of some activity on his station. The only lapses in the entire span of Proteus' tenure as city administrator.

"Nothing. None of your business. Who the hell are you?" Roger said.

Then he noticed the blasters hanging off her hip belt. *Strange attire for a hacker* he thought as he began to step away scanning the room for the AI's avatar. Singularity walked further into the office and looked around. The lights softened. The 1940 detective agency themed holograms returned, and this time, they seemed to radiate more solidly. Roger backed all the way to the far wall. He ducked for cover between a brown leather club chair and a dark oak coat rack. Singularity looked straight into the hidden camera behind the large desk in the center of the room.

"I like what you've done with the place," she said.

Proteus reappeared next to Singularity and gave her a warm smile.

"Roger, this is Singularity, Orbit Lives' most celebrated, and I'd say, most stealth hacker. Although I thought I could sense her poking around inside of my circuits for about a week. I did not know she was on Earth Space City One until this very moment."

"Nine days," she said. Singularity nodded towards the avatar and hustled towards the array of video terminals projecting the various angles of the tragic event Proteus had witnessed. Proteus immediately changed the video display to project the view of Earth from the City.

"Pro, I'm not liking any of this. First, you find me, then she shows up," Roger said.

"Relax Roger. I'm sure that she doesn't know it yet, but Ms. Singularity is here to help us understand the recent happenings."

"Happenings? What?" she said, turning to Proteus who shifted his avatar across the room so that he stood framed by the view of Earth from orbit. He relaxed the holographic metaphor at the same time and the room's usual stark white walls, floor, and ceiling reappeared. There was no furniture in the room. Just the two humans and the AI's avatar remained. Roger fidgeted with nowhere to hide, and Singularity swung around to face him.

"Wait," she said, "Roger? Roger Foster?"

"Maybe," he said as a sour look formed on his face. "So?"

"Oh, man, this is better than I could have imagined," Singularity said.

"What are you talking about?" Roger asked.

"It seems Miss Singularity is a bit of a fan of yours. She's worked hard collecting Roger Foster memorabilia," Proteus said.

"That's just weird," he said.

"A bit of a history buff, I'd say," Proteus said as his avatar materialized next to Roger.

"Creepy, I'd say. Will you stop jumping around and stay in one place, please," Roger said staring at the avatar's face for the first time since he entered the room.

"Why are you here?" Roger said to her.

Slightly flustered, she brushed it off and stood up straight. "I'm not here on Corporation business."

"Then, why are you here? No one wants you here."

"I like what you did to Harrington," Singularity said, ignoring his question. She moved up close to him so the three were all within a tight circle in the middle of the room. She looked straight at Roger who caught himself staring at her.

"I didn't do anything to anyone," he said.

"hmmm."

She poked him on the cheek, letting her finger linger in the flesh below his right eye an instant longer than she intended, surprised by the softness of his skin. Roger jumped back and glared at her.

"What the hell lady?" Roger said.

"Just making sure you're actually in this room and not some hologram. I didn't think you ever left Earth."

"I don't," Roger said. "This jerk hijacked my coffee bot to get me up here. He promised no one would ever know."

"No one did know," Proteus responded. "Ms. Singularity's presence here is a complete coincidence."

"Pro, you know better than that. Something's not right here. The Corporation is good, but not lucky enough to send her on a whim."

"They didn't. Ms. Singularity has been trying to get inside my core since Earth Space City Two went offline. I'm not sure The Corporation even knows what she's up to," Proteus said.

"When did ESC2 go offline?" Roger asked.

"Yesterday, officially. A month ago in reality," Singularity said.

"How?" he said, turning and winking at Proteus.

"That's what I'd like to know," she said, looking quizzically at Roger's action.

"Have you tried to reboot the station?" Roger asked Singularity as she took a step towards the screen.

"We've been trying. No one can get access to any of her systems to initiate a reboot. We can't even issue a shutdown. She seems stuck in an infinite loop," she said.

"Pro, I didn't think that was possible," Roger said, winking again.

"It's not. And please stop winking at me. Miss Singularity knows we know about Despina."

28

Dr. Helen Foster's monumental discovery in Artificial Intelligence computer processing involved reversing the philosophy behind wildly successful GANs--Generative Adversarial Networks. She created a paradigm where intelligence emerged from cooperative, rather than combative, activities. Each single AI entity Dr. Foster developed existed as a member of a community of interrelated, but unique, software agents. In this way, she established a system of mutating learning in an environment of shared beneficial monitoring in which each quantum-based software machine participated in a collective AI architecture. In essence, her creations, rather than expressing a survival of the fittest algorithm, evolved towards the survival of community.

No single AI, Proteus or his sister clone, Despina, was ever alone in their processing, yet each capable of articulating their individuality in a manner never seen before in computers. Despina should not have been able to enter an infinite loop, because community network of cooperating AIs would not allow it. Infinite loops provided no benefit to a community. Yet, she did. And, she did it without withdrawing from the network. Every one of Helen Foster AIs could sense Despina and talk to her, but none of her internal software agents chose to respond. Proteus' only conclusion was that his sister, in essence, was busy thinking about something that only she knew.

Roger turned to look at the display of outside the station that Proteus had been projecting since Singularity busted into the room. Yesterday, he had just pulled off the hack of a lifetime. Today he was mixed up in a Corporate drama. Never had a cup of coffee cost him so much.

"I have to get over there," he said. "Pro, can you get me in?"

"I'm not sure what you can do there that I haven't tried from here."

"I was there when you were being built. I added a back door to you that my mother never knew about. Despina might have that still active in her. I need to be in physical contact with her core to see."

"What back door?" Singularity said.

"Never mind," he said.

"Roger, there is no way you could have hidden a program in my circuitry that neither I nor your mother would not have noticed and eradicated."

"Just trust me. If I can get to City Two, I might be able to figure something out. Not just for Despina, but for your little issue, too."

"What is going on here?" Singularity said.

"Nothing," Proteus and Roger said in unison.

"Roger," Proteus said, "what did you do to me?"

"Forget it will you."

"I'd like to know, too," Singularity said.

"It was just some stupid code a 12-year-old who spent way too much time without adult supervision would write."

"I don't believe it," Proteus said.

"Neither do I," Singularity said.

"Seriously. We're going to do this?" Roger said.

"Yes," Singularity and Proteus said together.

"Ok. But, remember you asked for it."

Roger paused. He looked at Singularity and frowned. Her gaze only made him want to slide deeper behind his long red hair and disappear. The Proteus avatar seemed to glow more brightly as Roger contemplated his next action.

"Go on," she said.

"Fine!" he said. "Proteus, on Roger Dodger rocket man's command, execute directive 80085."

Proteus' avatar flickered. When it solidified, rather than wearing his brother Paul's face, Proteus appeared as his mother from Roger's childhood. The hologram stood erect, then slightly shifted its stance to lift the heel of its right foot off the ground and drop its left hip. A small, dark, holographic representation of a comic cloud appeared behind it and a one-second blast of a tugboat's foghorn filled the room. The avatar flickered and Proteus was back in control.

"Oh. Nice. That's not in my archive" Singularity said, bringing her hand up to cover her mouth and suppress a laugh.

"I was twelve. Wait, what archive?"

"Nothing, never mind," Singularity said, looking away.

"What happened? What did I miss?" Proteus asked.

"Nothing," Roger said, looking at Singularity. He turned back. "Now get me to Despina."

Proteus' avatar's face went blank for an instant. Roger noticed and realized that Proteus had accessed the office camera and saw what had happened. Proteus's avatar disappeared from the room.

"That's not going to happen again," Proteus disembodied voice said.

"I told you to let it go."

"The Corporation has been crawling all over the air space around ESC2 since it went offline. We're going to have to sneak on the station," Singularity said.

"We?" Roger said.

"You're not going anywhere without me, boy genius," Singularity said, still giggling.

"You are The Corporation," Roger said.

"I think Ms. Singularity might be willing to suspend her Corporate activities for a little while," Proteus said.

"There is something going on here that I need to understand. What was that incident you mentioned before?" she said.

"Just a camera malfunction in one of the airlocks down in one of the older neighborhoods," Proteus said.

"Camera malfunction?"

"Pro, don't."

"Roger, I think we can trust her."

"Why?"

"I've been watching her for several years. She's an unusual Corporate employee. You two aren't so very different. She might be willing to help us, I think."

Roger frowned as his older brother's image stood next to him with something resembling a smirk.

0x0B

"Did that really just happen?" Singularity stared at the frozen image of Dr. Helen Foster moments before the airlock door opened and she disappeared. In the instant blip before she looked up at the camera, she seemed to motion out the window towards where Earth Space City Two had been during its prior rotation. Proteus replayed the last few seconds of the woman's life. The three watched her look into the camera, smile, and vanish out of the airlock into the icy death of space.

Proteus' avatar glided towards Singularity. "I have not found any witnesses. All my inquiring of databases finds no match for the woman. There are no reports on any network sources about a missing person or even the structure of the Apollo Eleven Order. I can't locate a high priestess's arrival at the station. There is no physical human to match the image we just saw."

"Roger, was that your mother?" Singularity said.

"I am not sure. I haven't seen her in years," he said as the still image of the woman's face reappeared on the screen in front of him. The visual enhanced to tighten on her countenance, and her grin appeared ready to reveal the secrets of a mystery that she wasn't telling. Roger drifted towards the image of the woman who might have been his mother in the final seconds of her life.

"Proteus, any chance you have any recent photos of Helen Foster?" Singularity asked.

"My searches have only been able to acquire images of a woman in shadow."

"Can you run an aging algorithm on any clear photo you have

32

from her past?"

"I have tried. For some reason, I am unable to access any photos of Doctor Foster. There don't seem to be any."

Singularity looked back at the image on the monitor. Dr. Helen Foster's location remained hidden. All of her images erased. Yet, someone looking like her died in an accident on ESC1.

"What do you mean?" Singularity said.

"Her image has been completely wiped from all data stores. There are exactly zero photos of her remaining," Proteus said.

At that, Roger returned his attention to the others. He fidgeted back and forth. "That's not exactly true," he said, reaching into his pocket. He pulled out a cracked, faded leather wallet.

"What the hell is that?" Singularity asked.

"It was my grandfather's. My father gave it to me the Christmas before the explosion. I don't know why I've kept it." Roger gently unfolded the worn black pouch and slid out a tattered slip of paper. He handed it to Proteus. A family snapshot from Roger's childhood materialized on a monitor. It was a sepia-toned novelty photograph of his family dressed in American Western 1800 costumes on a vacation. Roger looked to be around four years old, dressed in a vest and dark wool pants. His brother held an old Winchester lever-action rifle. His father wore a stiff ten-gallon hat tilted to the left with a pair of six-guns strapped around his waist. His mother adorned a simple dark Edwardian woman's suit. All four of them displayed grins as if they were trying very hard to hide their giggles behind the outfits.

Proteus let the image linger for several seconds before zooming in on the face of a seated woman surrounded by two boys and a man. On another screen, Proteus age-progressed Helen Foster's face. Roger stood transfixed as his mother's image softened with the visual effects of time. He saw the face of the woman who disappeared from his life transform into the face of a woman he no longer knew.

"Holy shit," Solidarity said when Proteus stopped the algorithm and slid the two nearly identical images next to each other.

"Pro, what the fuck?"

"99.9997% match," Proteus said. His avatar slid across the room to take a closer look at the two images side-by-side. "There is something peculiar about this."

"Yeah, like all of it," Roger said.

"I mean, the images are too exact. Random pixels correlate across the whole photograph," Proteus said.

"Roger, did your mother know you had that picture?" Singularity asked.

"I guess. She gave it to me on that same Christmas to put in the wallet."

"Could she have known that you'd have it all this time?" Proteus asked.

"Pro, are you saying she set this up years ago?" Roger said.

"Not necessarily set it up. But she could have taken a guess that you'd still have the wallet with the photograph," Proteus said.

"For what reason? Do the correlating pixels make any meaningful pattern?" Singularity asked.

"I think she wanted me to come here and see Proteus," Roger said.

"That is what I think, too, but Roger we have a problem," said Proteus.

"What?"

"The Corporation is here."

"Pro, I'm getting tired of you getting surprised by shit," Roger said.

"What do you mean, Proteus?" Solidarity asked.

"I mean what I said. A troop of Corporation officers has just arrived at the level D ship bay. I am talking with their captain right now. They are on their way here." Proteus said.

All but one of the monitors in the office adjusted to display the outside of the station from different angles. On the remaining screen, a Corporate Captain walked next to Proteus' avatar down the corridor leading to the elevator shaft that would take them to the core of the city and the office where the three were currently talking.

"What do they want? Stall them," Roger said.

"Sheldon!" Singularity said, her shoulders stiffening at the sight of the man leading the way. "He can't stall them. If Proteus acts in any way that is not 100% normal protocol, Sheldon will know something is up." Singularity said. "Let him come. We have to get out of here."

"We?" Roger said.

"Now!" Singularity said.

A door on the opposite wall of the main door opened.

"Roger. It was good to see you. Go with her. Talk to Despina."

The two humans dashed out of the room as the office hologram shifted to the Corporate standard gray and blue. Roger and Singularity escaped, and Proteus' avatar faded. Less than a second later in the hallway outside, Proteus' avatar deliberately invited Captain Sheldon to enter the office.

"As I told you. I have not seen Helen Foster in years. It is likely that when she constructed my core, she implemented a means to keep me unaware of her movements."

"That's why I'm here. All of her images have disappeared. Not only did she physically disappear twenty years ago, but now we have just realized that all of her images were wiped. It's as if she has never existed."

"When did you first notice this?" Proteus asked.

"Singularity, one of our operatives discovered it and reported it to me yesterday," Sheldon said.

"I'd like to hear more about this discovery of hers," Proteus said.

"Yes, I would, too. Unfortunately, she has gone dark. Which is what she does when she is on to something. I have to wait until I hear from her again. Of course, you probably know that and everything else we have spoken about since I've arrived."

"I do have access to most existing data systems. My programming dictates that I never presume to share more than I have been told by a human. But, then, you know that," Proteus said.

Sheldon wondered why this AI had not been decommissioned yet. It was probably because as the oldest city in the fleet, ESC1 and its inhabitants, drew very little interest from The

Corporation, and that stupid old sap Harrington was nostalgic. He was going to fix that. He was going to fix the whole system.

"Tell me where Singularity is right now," Sheldon said.

"Ms. Singularity is a brilliant hacker. She knows how to stay out of view."

"Administrator Proteus, I gave you a direct order, yet you did not give me an exact answer," Sheldon said.

"I'm sorry, Sir. I will run a diagnostic immediately," Proteus said.

"First answer my question. Do you know the exact location of Singularity?" Sheldon said.

"The exact location? No," Proteus said.

"Do you know where she is headed?" Sheldon said.

Proteus paused for 3 microseconds, a tell-tale give-away for an AI. If Captain Sheldon noticed, he didn't let on.

"I am sorry, Sir. I do not." Proteus was programmed never to lie. Technically, the fact that he helped her escape but did not at that moment know her exact intentions did not constitute an answer that was outside his parameters of truthfulness. That seemed a new assessment of his operating instructions. He'd put a record of this interaction away for later analysis.

"Can you find her?" the Captain said.

"I have already started looking, but as I said, Ms. Singularity knows how to hide her tracks."

Again, still technically a true response. Proteus searched his core for another gap in his programming that would allow him to fully lie to Sheldon.

"Bring up the cameras on the upper levels of the city. I want a complete view of the surrounding activity." The monitors immediately changed to display Earth Space City One from every angle emanating from the communication spire at the top of the station. The view revealed space ships, maintenance bots, and shuttles moving around the city like a swarm of bees.

After a moment, Sheldon pointed at the corner of one display. A single, aged, two-seat vacation class cruiser moved slowly away from the city. Proteus zoomed the display to focus on the ragged vehicle. "Can you give me the details on the people in that ship?"

"Arthur Sampson and his wife traveling to ESC7. Their first vacation in twelve years. The ship, Erica's Inheritance, registered to Wendell Dobson, Arthur's childhood friend. They have a licensed transfer for a trip to ESC7, ESC12, and a two day stay on Earth."

"Get me a visual of the inside," Sheldon said.

"There are four cameras onboard the ship. Which one do you want?"

"All of them!" Sheldon said.

A look of annoyance flashed across Captain Sheldon's face as he moved closer to the wall of monitors. Proteus's avatar blinked out of existence. He reappeared behind Sheldon as the feeds from all the cameras splashed on to the screens. One screen showed two humans from behind and another showed them from the front. They were seated in battered leather recliners dressed in travel space suits with helmets and full-face masks, a common habit for humans who travelled infrequently in space away from their home station.

"Zoom in on the visors," Sheldon said, "and, get me a feed from their HUDs inside those helmets!"

The visors obscured the traveler's faces as the heads-up-display on each helmet flickered with activity. One large monitor in Proteus' office exploded with images of oranges and cherries spinning on a virtual slot machine--the man's helmet. The other screen broadcasted products from jewelry and clothing catalogs.

Sheldon turned and headed for the door.

"I want a full report on your diagnostics, and I will be sending a technician to inspect your core."

If the door had been mounted on hinges, Captain Sheldon would have ripped it off the wall. Instead, a gentle swish signified his rapid departure from the office. His ship and crew left the city as swiftly and silently as they arrived.

Proteus watched as the bulk of the armada eventually retreated from his monitor.

The Paul Foster avatar disappeared as the office flickered back to the dark oak 1940 detective hologram he preferred. The images on the monitors dissolved leaving the one with the craft that drew Sheldon's attention. Proteus calculated the chances that he had noticed it was heading away from ESC7 not towards it. The odds were not in their favor. Sheldon's coterie contained too much intel for him to miss the small detail. The hedge depended upon whether Sheldon considered the likelihood of a vacationing couple taking a scenic route. There was an excellent chance Singularity knew what Sheldon would do and make allowances. As if on cue, the small craft modified its course to include a drive-by of several captured ice asteroids tourists usually visit on holiday. While Roger was new to traveling around the city-wide system, Singularity was not--she was a pro.

It was only then that he considered what Captain Sheldon said about Singularity being the one who discovered that Helen Foster's image had been wiped from history. Proteus' avatar reappeared and sat behind the virtual desk to run some calculations, but there were too many variables to generate any results with high confidence. He could only simulate the parameters necessary to know if Roger was capable of handling what was going on ESC2, if Despina had closed his back door, or if he was right about Singularity's motivations.

It was too late to change what he had just set into motion.

0x0C

Roger was staring out the cruiser's main window at The Corporation's military vessels surrounding ESC1 when he noticed the tiny LED indicator flicker on and off revealing that someone was in the process of scanning the ship. He assumed it was Proteus under direct instructions from The Corporation's officer, most likely Captain Sheldon. Roger was not sure what Proteus would be able to do to hide their identity and the cruiser's manifest. They left quickly on a ship Proteus had reserved for them under assumed names in a remote rental launch bay located several decks below where Sheldon had made his entrance.

Singularity saw the light, too, and tried to let her shoulders relax into the seat, appearing as casual as possible. She and Roger posed as a couple headed out for a once-in-a-lifetime vacation. With her custom unregistered holographic mask in place, Singularity was confident that Sheldon would be unable to recognize her. She hoped Roger's mask was good enough to pass the in-visor scan that was sure to come. Turning towards and into him to prevent direct scrutiny of her mask, she affectionately reached out and took hold of his hand. If he wasn't expecting the gesture, he didn't show it. In response, Roger grasped Singularity's hand and leaned towards her. He smiled. She smiled back. A happy couple. Roger let go and shifted back to steering the cruiser. Singularity dropped back into her seat, keeping the angle of her mask away from all of the onboard cameras.

She tried not to look too obvious as she visually interrogated the armada of warships that always accompanied Sheldon. She assumed Scoundrel was on one of them and running his own scans, attempting to hack the cruiser's navigation system and internal cameras. Proteus had to provide enough access to fool Scoundrel's scanners, giving the impression that the ship was wide open to him but not enough to expose who was actually on it. As Roger and Singularity's cruiser passed a side window of the command vessel, she spied Scoundrel staring at them. She kept him in her periphery, her gaze still on Roger, pretending not to notice the array of heavily armed battleships surrounding them as they headed away from the city.

Scoundrel twittered between peering out the window and looking down at his comm. Singularity had kept a number of secret unregistered holomasks, and she was hoping its physique blocking software was subtle enough to not raise any flags. She hoped that he'd not detect anything to pique his curiosity. There were always ships coming and going from ESC1. He'd scan them all to find the one most likely to contain her. Roger's presence was more than useful. Scoundrel and Sheldon wouldn't have known they should be looking for a couple. After a few moments, he looked back up at the cruiser passing the window and turned away and walked out of view.

The LED flickered once again indicating that the scan was over as Roger maneuvered the cruiser past the formation of military vessels and punched in the navigation instructions towards ESC7. As the cruiser responded to the new coordinates, the armada began disassembling in preparation for moving on.

"That went ok. Let's hope we're clear," Singularity said, pulling her hand away.

"It seems like it. Although, I'm not sure why Proteus has a ship with a clouded manifest. I need to talk to him about that when I get back."

"It does seem strange for an AI," Singularity said.

"He is not like other AI's," Roger said, dropping his visor, but keeping his mask engaged.

"How do you know?" Singularity said.

"When I was a kid, I watched her. Helen spent countless hours talking to him. Whispering to him. She was obsessed, nearly hysterical, but focused like she was preparing him for something."

"That must have been weird to watch your mother like that," she said.

"Losing my father and brother at the age of 12 was weird. That woman was just crazy. Families are over-rated," he said.

"I'm sure she had something in mind. You don't just abandon your child," she said.

"Proteus was her child, too. In many ways, he was just an infant and needed more attention," he said.

"A quantum-powered, all-knowing, first-of-his-kind infant," she said.

"It doesn't matter. I've been making my own way. Doing ok, if you ask me," Roger said.

"You mean, breaking the law. Hacking Orbit Lives. Stuff like that," she said.

Singularity swiped her hand in front of her and the news broadcast about the Harrington heist that had been playing on a small screen in the lounge area of the cruiser jumped to the main monitor in front of them.

Roger swiveled his seat to face her.

"I do no worse than what was done to me. Better, in fact, because my targets deserve what they get," Roger said.

"A noble thief," Singularity said.

Roger waved his hand and the news broadcast shrunk to a dot in the center of the monitor, replaced with a growing image of an enormous space city above Earth.

"How long do we have to pretend to head to ESC7 before we can go to Despina?" Roger said.

"It depends on how much Sheldon trust me. I'm guessing not much right now," Singularity said.

"Why do you say that?" Roger said.

"Scoundrel's demigod just launched off the Corporate command battleship. He's following us," Singularity said, looking down at her personal comm.

"Great. Scoundrel? Is there something you want to tell me? First, you show up, then The Corporation. Now Scoundrel is personally involved. This seems like a lot of heat on me for a simple hack. Harrington's got insurance. They'll let the people enjoy themselves for a few days and then take it all back. No real harm. Just an embarrassment on their cyber-security team," he said.

"They don't care about Harrington, or you. They're after me," Singularity said.

"What did you do?" he said.

"Nothing. I just ditched Scoundrel on ESC21," she said.

"ESC21? Must be more than that," he said.

"A Corporate item got lost. They think I have it," she said.

"What item? Do you have it?" Roger said, glaring at her.

"Yeah. I got it," Singularity said, thumbing on her comm without acknowledging his stare.

"If you dragged me and Proteus into some Corporate bullshit...," Roger said.

"I can handle it," she said.

"What the hell is going on?" Roger said.

"Relax. We'll just lay low on ESC7 for a couple of days. Everything will be fine. Then we'll investigate Despina," Singularity said.

"I don't know how much time Proteus has before The Corporation finds an excuse to retire him. And, I'm not sure how relaxing it'll be with Scoundrel on our tail," Roger said.

"I can handle Scoundrel. Just be prepared to access Despina when we get to ESC2."

"Don't worry about me," Roger said, reaching across Singularity to a large black knob on the dashboard in front of her. In one move, he spun it and slammed down hard. The panel next to him opened revealing a steaming cup of chai latte. "Damn it," he muttered under his breath.

Singularity smiled without looking up from her comm. Her thumbs were a blur on the keypad. Roger stood, grabbed the steaming mug, and went to the cruiser's lounge. He put his drink down on the table and dropped to the couch, facing away from Singularity, crossing his arms like a child. She never let on that she was watching him, even as he began massaging his palm from where he burnt it on the hot mug.

Singularity's holo-mask was programmed to display only happy faces. If Roger was able to see her actual face, he might have noticed a flash of concern that quickly gave way to a stone-cold stare. She wasn't sure what Proteus had been able to do or what Sheldon had guessed. Scoundrel was watching them. They were going to have to get to ESC2 another way. Sheldon gave her a long leash, but she had learned over the years that it was always a leash.

0x0D

The cruiser approached ESC7 like every other holiday traveler does--too slow and erratic. Being new to space flight, Roger cautiously performed the maneuvers to their berth under the patient direction of the city's space control, trying to blend in. He quickly picked up how to maneuver the ship's helm, but didn't let on. He enjoyed watching Singularity's nervousness. He could tell she was on the edge of her seat, ready to grab the controls from him at any moment.

The red scanning indicator burned solid while they were in the vicinity of a city. Singularity sat in the passenger's seat, swiveled away from the front window, hidden from direct view, one eye on Roger, the other monitoring Scoundrel's movements on her comm. The Corporate hacker-spy kept his ship just out of the city's scanning range, but close enough for his technology to track their cruiser's location.

After they set the cruiser down on the busy tarmac, Roger and Singularity disembarked. They each carried a brand new suitcase they had found in the cruiser's berth--another issue Roger was going to talk to Proteus about--there seemed to have been too much preparation for their impromptu meeting and emergency departure. A valet from the ESC7 Grand Hotel ran to greet them with a bellhop in tow.

"Thank you for joining us on your vacation. I'm Charles. Let me know if you need anything," he said extending a key card to them as he bowed. He remained in the bow until Singularity pointed her comm at him. A small ping indicated a tip had been transferred, and Charles retreated with a nod.

"Follow Anthony to the hotel shuttle. I will stow your ship."

Within minutes, Roger and Singularity were sliding past the lush, expansive interior of Earth Space City Seven in an open maglev vehicle. They felt the simulated tropical humidity embrace their skin. ESC7's vacation facilities had recently been revitalized to imitate an Earth equatorial paradise. There was a two-year-long waiting list for access and a perfect place to get lost in. Once again, Proteus had planned well Roger thought.

As they sped through the large domed area, Roger shifted in his seat, constantly scanning for trouble.

"Just relax. Remember, we're on vacation," Singularity said, taking his arm.

"Something is not right," he said.

"Yeah, this is too easy. There should be at least some Orbit Lives military presence here," she said.

"Anthony, how long to the hotel?" Roger asked the driver, leaning forward.

"Just a few more minutes, sir," he said.

"Can you take us to a cafe first? You can take our bags to our room and we'll follow on later," Singularity said.

"The hotel has a wonderful cafe," he said.

"Someplace quiet and out of the way," Singularity said as she pointed her comm at Anthony and released a sizeable tip.

"I know just the place," he said, slowing to turn off the main passage. The driver looked cautiously around before banking hard to the left down an alley overgrown with jungle vines. He pulled close to the edge to let traffic pass, then continued down a secluded side street. As they proceeded deeper into the labyrinth of streets, the verdant growth of the main avenues was replaced by browns and greys. An occasional gloomy lamp light revealed random groups of humans or bots lingering in the shadows. Roger wasn't sure if he was witnessing a simulated seediness or an actual squalid underworld.

The car stopped in front of a building with no signage and no one lurking outside. Singularity tipped the driver again, and she led Roger to the building's actual wooden door.

Singularity opened the door and walked in like she owned the place. Roger took a moment to look inside before he decided whether he should follow her. Light spilled onto the street. She reached back and grabbed his wrist, pulling him in. A robotic bouncer slid down from above and behind them and shut the door from the outside.

"We're safe here," she said. Roger looked uncertain as a hush dropped over the room. The bar was full of patrons who slowly turned back to their conversations, most of them still keeping their eyes on the newcomers.

The crowd in the middle of the place parted. A short, round woman wearing an apron, holding a knife in her one mechanical arm, walked up to them.

"Who's this now? No holos allowed. Drop the masks," she said.

"Hey, Rita," Singularity said, leaning her face down, close so the woman could get a good look. She dropped her disguise for an instant, revealing her identity, and the old woman gave her a slight grin.

"Nici," Rita said, "I wondered when you'd get back here."

"You never know. Is the room empty?" Singularity said.

"Right where you left it," Rita said, turning to make her way back to the kitchen.

Singularity motioned to Roger to follow her and headed for a doorway at the back of the room where another large robot bouncer stood sentry. She stopped and let it scan her.

"He's with me," she said, pointing over her shoulder at Roger.

The bouncer lifted his arm and let them pass through the doorway. It led down a dimly lit hall of closed, painted doors. At the end, on the left, a green door slid open inward as they approached. She pushed through with Roger in tow.

The room was small, about the size of an infant's bedroom. In the center was a table with four chairs, illuminated by a single yellow-bulb light on a chain.

"Rita has a flair for the dramatic," Singularity said. Then, to the room, she ordered, "default settings." The table and chairs disappeared. In their place materialized two contemporary reclining chairs. A soft white light began to radiate from the top edge of the walls as the hanging lamp dissolved. As sideboard slid out from the back wall with a comm center and chair.

"How'd you?..." Roger started.

"I used to come here a lot," she said.

"A Corporate spy command center?" he said.

"More like my secret hide-away. From a previous life." Singularity sat down in one of the chairs as a comm appeared. She tapped on the keypad and brought up the display.

"Let's see if we can find those Corporate goons that I know are hiding around here somewhere."

Roger sat down next to her, fingers itching to grab the haptic user interface. Singularity noticed.

"Calm down cyber-thief. The controls are DNA matched to me. You stick your fingers in where they don't belong and you'll get a nasty shock."

Roger sank back into his seat, dejected. "This sucks." He stood up and began to pace around the room as Singularity worked the controls.

"It's worse than I thought. We have elite agents crawling all over this place," she said.

"Sheldon really doesn't trust you," Roger said.

"I'm thinking it's probably Scoundrel. After what I did to him, I'm sure he'd love to see me in jail."

"What the heck kind of Corporate soap opera have you got me mixed up in?"

"Don't worry. Right now, we have to get out of here, off this station, and on to ESC2," Singularity said, standing up to join Roger pacing. When Roger noticed that they both were pacing, he dropped into one of the recliners.

"Does this joint have a news monitor?"

"News," Singularity said to the room's voice interface and the wall in front of Roger exposed four different news channels.

A blurred photo captured from the main terminal on ESC1 flashed up on one of the screens. A red circle surrounded Roger's current holomask.

"This is not good," Roger said.

"That's just your mask. Do you know what is worse?" Singularity said as she waved her hand over her comm. The wall monitors changed to show a map of the city with their location in the center. Dozens of red dots gathered and slowly moved towards them, closing in on the alley.

"Those blips are Corporate soldiers. Someone knows we're here," she said.

"Nice friends you have. The old hag sold us out," Roger said.

Rita burst into the room. "You have to go. My kids told me there is a massive Corporate movement closing in," she said.

Roger and Singularity looked at her, then up at the map on the wall.

"Oh, you already know," Rita said.

"Stairs," Singularity said to the room. Opposite the monitors, a doorway appeared with stairs leading down. Singularity gave Rita a kiss on the cheek, and the two dashed out the stairwell. The room returned to its pre-Singularity state as Rita walked back into her bar ready to stonewall whoever walked through the front door.

0x0E

Proteus's avatar moved around his office. While he was doing this, other versions of his avatar paced up and down several of the less populated hallways on ESC1. Images of him pacing around ESC1 were plastered across the monitors in his office. At the moment he was deep in thought about his current situation, his avatar haunted the halls of Earth Space City One. It was part of his process. There was nothing within the domain of his city that he couldn't control. But, letting the photo get accessed by Scoundrel introduced a variable that he hadn't expected and couldn't control. He had to trust, if an AI can do anything but trust, that Roger and Singularity would know that it was he who gave Scoundrel the breadcrumbs to the photo. He took the chance that they would figure out what to do next.

Sheldon's appearance at Proteus' office revealed more than a glitch in his software. The unexplained death of an unidentified nun who looked exactly like the mother of modern artificial intelligence and an Earth-bound cyber-criminal being tracked across the network of space cities at the same time seemed too outlandish to be merely a coincidence. Then throw in Singularity's involvement. The whole thing had to have a deeper significance. Something transcendent was happening, and the answer may be within Despina's infinite loop. Roger and Singularity had to get there and figure it out.

For Proteus' part in this, it was not difficult to discover Scoundrel's attempts at accessing ESC1's network. Compared to Singularity's subtle pokes, prods and misdirection, Scoundrel's attempted intrusions banged away against Proteus' security protocols like a toddler's mallet playing whack-a-mole. In fact, Proteus had to rewrite a number of security protocols on the fly in order to mask his knowledge of Scoundrel's attempts. He gave him breadcrumbs, but no real information.

While keeping Scoundrel occupied, Proteus also continued to analyze the airlock video and the surrounding footage. The more he worked the files, the more it seemed that the video was downloaded directly into his memory--that there was no actual woman in the airlock. The video was a plant, or a message, or a warning. A phantom. He had finally accepted that.

His analysis changed to figuring out how it got there and why. Singularity could have done it, but that didn't make sense. As far as he knew, there was no other Corporate hacker who had the ability to swap his live feed with a simulated file. Nor was there any reason for The Corporation to play games with him--they could just replace him. No questions asked.

And why use Helen Foster's image?

0x0F

Captain Jason Sheldon didn't often listen to Scoundrel, especially where Singularity was concerned. He knew of their time together on ESC21. He also knew of Scoundrel's petty jealousy of Singularity's skill. Yet, this time, she left him no choice. She shouldn't have taken the quantum entanglement dot. It contained the only secret Sheldon had ever kept from her, but it was the big one--his plan to lead an Orbit Lives' take-over of Earth's government so he could limit the ever-growing ability of artificial intelligent machines. Sheldon never liked working for The Corporation. But, he saw it as a necessary part to play, to do what he thought was right for humanity's future.

To that end, what mattered most to Sheldon was keeping a low profile--efficiently and completely. And, to do that, regardless of how he felt about The Corporation, he needed Scoundrel to carry out his orders.

At least Scoundrel was predictable. The only wildcard, and not an insignificant wildcard, in the whole scenario, was Singularity, and she had the dot. Scoundrel had followed her to ESC1 and lost her. Sheldon knew that Singularity was playing with both him and Scoundrel. Counting on that fact remained his only chance of recovering the dot before she realized what it represented.

When Scoundrel left the command ship, Sheldon isolated himself in his office. On a completely private and secure network, he kept a secret, isolated clone of the Proteus AI. He had no appreciation for the cooperative nature that Dr. Foster built into Proteus. His Proteus clone was tamed, slightly buggy, yet still a derivative of the most power AI entity ever created.

It was a challenge to create and maintain a personal copy when The Corporation assumed Dr. Foster's work. After the explosion, Helen had disappeared. The other Fosters, including Roger, were dead. In the chaos of the early days of Foster's disappearance and the shuffle to lock down her work, Sheldon secretly confiscated a relatively up-to-date snap-shot of Proteus' core backup. It took him nearly two years to acquire and assemble the hardware necessary to create his personal version of Proteus. And, it took a few more years for him to understand enough of the revolutionary algorithms and code that made it work. Sheldon even added his own tweaks to hide the truth of the AI's origin from itself. The one thing he couldn't do, no matter how many hours he spent on it, was change the Avatar from Paul Foster. So, he disabled it. It was much easier to give orders to a closet of computer components than a facsimile of his one-time friend, the man he had killed.

0x10

"Where are we going to go?" Roger grabbed Singularity's arm to stop her. She turned sharply toward him.

"We have to get off this station," she said, looking past him to see if they were being followed. The passage was quiet. The lights behind and ahead were just bright enough to provide faint shadows revealing no clear location or direction.

"How are we going to do that? I don't have another holomask," Roger said.

"We won't need them. They are already looking for us," Singularity said.

"That's comforting," he said.

"Come on. We can't stand around," she said.

Singularity took Roger's hand and pulled him down the passage, away from the Corporate soldiers. She knew Rita could stall them, but they were going to find the room and eventually the stairs. Her tech was good, and she was the best, but military tech was good enough to track two fugitives without much of a head start. And, if Scoundrel had posted Roger's mask across the solar system, then he knew finding that mask would lead to Singularity and the dot.

0x11

They hurried along the passage until Singularity slowed at an intersection. To the right, the hall was dark, but she entered the space without hesitation, Roger in tow. He gave little resistance, proceeding behind her, keeping pace with his eyes closed against the danger he could not see. Within a few strides, she raised Roger's hand and pushed it against a thin ladder rail going up.

"Climb," Singularity said.

Without hesitation, he found the first foothold and began ascending into the pitch-black above him.

Stopping after several minutes, he paused, looked down for her in the darkness, and said, "I sure hope you know what you're doing."

"Ten more feet. There's a landing to your left. Step in," she said

"How do you know all this?" he said.

"I've spent a lot of time here. Now, let's go." As she said that, footsteps and shouts from below echoed around them. Looking down, Roger saw flashlight beams flickering.

"How'd they find us?" Roger said.

"Just go. Get on the landing and try to keep quiet."

Roger leapt off the ladder and waited for Singularity to join him.

She stepped on to the platform and leaned in, pressing him against the wall. He could taste her breath. There was something familiar about it. It was organic, of Earth, not mechanical like most people who have spent theirs lives in space breathing canned air. She reached around him and found a lever just below the small of his back.

"As soon as I open this door, they are going to know exactly where we are. Follow me, move quickly, and stay close," Singularity said.

She slid the handle and pushed the door in. A wave of brilliant chaos blinded Roger. The sound from the soldiers below exploded. Flashlight beams and laser trails saturated the ladder shaft behind them.

Singularity sprinted across what appeared to be a high-end women's intimates store. He bolted after her, crashing past displays of camisoles, bras, and frilly nighties. Perfect holographic models flickered in his wake, unaware of the intruders passing through them. Luckily, they arrived in the middle of a holiday sale. The store looked more like a Mardi Gras party than a luxury boutique. The scene was complete when the soldiers arrived waving their weapons around, shouting at each other.

0x12

Back on ESC1, Proteus' avatars had stopped pacing. A single Paul Foster facsimile stood in the center of his office. He preferred to use the avatar even when he was alone. He slowly rotated around the room, inspecting dozens of monitors displayed across every inch of available wall space. The ceiling and floors were replaced with views of up and down scenes outside the station. An observer walking in on Proteus would see him leisurely revolving, suspended in space. They would not see the frantic activity taking place inside of him. He used every spare CPU cycle running simulations, analyzing video data, and interrogating his codebase and data files.

Several times a second, he followed lines of inquiry that abruptly ended at a glimpse of a sensation of almost an answer, if AIs were able to have glimpses or sensation. But the moments were fleeting as if he was looking at an echo of a moment, a false image on his periphery. Which was impossible since his avatar's eyes didn't have periphery. It took him several million simulations to realize the effect was being caused by his code redirecting itself as quickly, or slightly less quickly, or intentionally less quickly, avoiding each answer, since the sensation that he almost had left a faintly perceptible shadow.

"Curious," Proteus said aloud to nobody, returning to the floor of the room, replacing all of the displays with a soft white glow. On the center of one wall, a monitor appeared with the face of 12-year-old Roger Foster.

Proteus sometimes talked to this program that he created from his memory of Roger before the explosion. It was a merging of his core program and a randomly generated simulacrum of the Roger he remembered before the actual adult Roger appeared in his office hours before.

"What do you think?" Proteus said to the image on the screen.

"Not much to go on," the teenage Roger replied.

"Not much, indeed, but ... something. Something is definitely there. Or, should I say, not there," Proteus said.

"What are you talking about?" Roger said.

"I keep finding erasures and voids," Proteus said.

"Maybe you're just getting old," Roger said.

"I have a fully adaptive core. I don't get old," Proteus said.

"Then, you're drunk from too much data?" Roger said.

"I'm the most advanced... wait? what did you say?" Proteus said.

"Too much data is making you dopey," the animated Roger said, sticking his tongue out and crossing his eyes.

"No. Not the data part, the drunk part," Proteus said.

Roger faded. Proteus' avatar disappeared, and the office went dark. Lights in unpopulated sections of Earth Space City One dimmed. The temperature across the entire city fell a tenth of a degree as Proteus shifted as much power as he could to his core.

Simulations needed to be executed.

0x13

It wasn't often that Roger found himself in a store among women's underpants. He spent most of his life laying low, out of the public eye. He hardly even went into men's stores. This particular establishment was located in the most populated area of the largest tourist shopping center on ESC7. Security sirens erupted, igniting spinning red safety lights across the entire mall complex as he and Singularity darted past surveillance cameras. There seemed to be no place to hide. Local law enforcement scrambled out of every conceivable crevasse like thirsty frat boys to a kegger, and luckily for the two taking refuge among the bras, they were just as organized.

Singularity deftly maneuvered around both shoppers and police equally. Roger slightly less so. He had to stop himself from apologizing for every bump, knock, and spilled parcel in an effort to keep up with her. She made it to a maintenance hatch behind a series of vending machines and waited for him to catch up. As soon as he arrived, she grabbed the scruff of his neck and used his momentum to shove him through the hatch.

"Wait here," she said closing the door. She shattered the electric lock with the butt of one of her blasters, sealing him inside. At least a few minutes would pass before anyone was able to get at him. Singularity hoped that it was enough time to do what she needed to redirect the police's and Corporate soldier's attention.

The first policeman reached her. She ran at him, slid under his outstretched arms, snatched his weapon from his hand, and threw it across the floor into the frantic crowd. In one move, she stood up and flipped him hard enough to render him unconscious. Moments later, when two more security officers appeared, she was gone.

Roger found himself sitting in darkness. After being thrown to the ground by Singularity, he let his body relax into its stillness. He finally allowed himself to shift and unfold. He hesitated to use his comm as a flashlight for fear of giving away his location. So, Roger sat in the dark, waiting for Singularity. He wasn't sure how long he was going to be there, or if she was even going to actually return.

This was the first time he was alone since entering Proteus' office several hours before. He took a few moments to recount the incidents that had happened since he escaped Sheldon's grasp on ESC1 with Singularity. This time had been a whirlwind. The speed with which things went south bothered him. His crime, cyber-hacking Harrington, was nothing. Lowly Corporate employees would enjoy two days of revelry before the money was transferred back.

More-than-likely, to save face, Harrington would forgive his employee's indiscretions and no one would get punished. The whole event would be written off as a stunt to give some well-deserving workers an early holiday bonus. Roger had even sent a copy of an announcement email to Harrington's publicity agency. A week, tops, before everyone forgot about it, and the news moved on to other events.

The Corporate response on Singularity's digressions, too, based on what she said, seemed too severe. There must be something more at stake. Scoundrel was no Singularity, but he wasn't no one. He was good. And, he was tenacious, particularly when he thought his reputation was on the line. The only other time he felt so much heat was when Scoundrel caught a whiff of another caper Roger had in the works. He abandoned it to slip away. He wasn't sure if Scoundrel ever made the connection to him, but it took almost a full year to completely hide his trail. The guy didn't like to lose. It must really suck living in Singularity's shadow the way he did.

She must have been on to something really important for all

this mayhem he thought to himself as the maintenance hatch opened, filling the tiny closet with light. Instantly, Roger missed the darkness. He closed his eyes, hoping no one would see him.

"Let's go," Singularity said throwing a holomask at him. She turned away and headed off.

"Damn," he muttered under his breath, putting on the mask and activating it.

"Keep close," she said as they disappeared into the crowd undeterred by all the commotion from their holiday shopping. The sirens in their immediate area muted as red lights and warnings exploded on the other side of the shopping center. Singularity's diversion had begun, and from all appearances, it worked perfectly.

She led Roger back through the racks of nighties and camisoles to the central shaft where they had originally arrived. A complete dark silence greeted them as she leaned out to listen. She was on the ladder continuing up before Roger had a chance to catch his breath. Sighing, and after a beleaguered look around the boutique that had returned to its own holiday craziness, he scrambled up after her.

0x14

Singularity peered around the open hatchway looking for movement. When she saw none, she motioned to Roger to follow her. They were in the commercial shipping bay of ESC7, the center of activity for keeping the city and its visitors in supplies, both legal and illicit. Ships came and went incessantly, keeping the city operating in all ways that a vacation resort needed to operate.

Singularity spied what she was looking for.

She pulled Roger along the back wall until they got to *The Venture*, a mid-sized, aging supply tug crewed by hackers and outlaws. Captain Fancy never turned down a drink, a supply run, a covert op that paid, or a request from Singularity. Today was his lucky day--he was going to get all four.

"Lookout Cap." Wally Sour, both hacker and outlaw, unloading crates from the hold, saw Singularity first. He immediately realized his mistake. She was on him in no time. She had his mouth covered with one hand and the business end of a blaster poking his ribs with the other.

"You say my name, and I will kill you," she said.

"Ah, shoot. I wasn't going to do that," he mumbled through her embrace. She kissed him on the cheek as he squirmed in her grasp. Captain Fancy had walked over to inspect the activity outside his ship. She let go of Sour and turned to face him.

"You have room for two more?" she asked.

"Looking for work?" Fancy said.

"We'll do what it takes to get off this dump as soon as

possible," she said, handing him a small flask. He looked long at the bottle in her hand but eventually took it. He turned back to his crew who had witnessed the whole scene.

"Sour, we leave in five," Fancy said.

"There's more for you if you make it one," Singularity said.

"You heard her," Fancy said.

"Aye-aye, Cap," Sour said.

Roger jumped in to help Sour unload the rest of the crates. When they were done, Roger disappeared into *The Venture* while Sour quickly filed the manifest. They were departing the shipping bay on ESC7 in less than seventy seconds.

There were six crew in total on *The Venture*, Fancy and Sour, the Palmer twins--Eli and Elf--the ship's muscle, the cook Johnson, and the navigator, Mute. All of them were seated around the large dining room table, set for a good luck toast ritual that preceded every voyage. Eli and Elf took up one whole long side of the table themselves. The identical twins were enormous men with large round faces. Each had a crop of black hair folded across their otherwise bald heads. Eli's flopped left, Elf's right. Otherwise, they were impossible to tell apart. So much so that the rest of the crew just took to calling either one of them "Twin" when they saw one of them without the other, which was rare. Off the ship, they worked together as a notorious hacker named "Miniscule." No one, except the crew of *The Venture*, knew Minuscule's true identity. They kept safe harbor onboard *The Venture* as long as they never hacked. Captain Fancy gave them respite but never allowed them to commit any cyber-crimes from any traceable location on or near the ship. That was fine with the Palmer Twins--they had been on a hacker holiday for several months and happy to be space-side.

Sour was a small-time criminal, space-port wharf-rat who wasn't very good at being either a criminal or a rat. He stuck around *The Venture* and Captain Fancy since it beat spending time in space city jails. Sour kept a low profile, at least tried, and in every run gave a brief ceremony of gratitude for the opportunity to be crewed on *The Venture*.

Captain Fancy had a way of keeping people safe and hidden.

There were even rumors that he was ex-Corporation, still with connections. Everyone expected that Singularity knew the truth, but she never talked about it. She is where they all went to keep their secrets. No one ever asked.

Singularity entered the room with Roger right behind her. As soon as he saw them, Johnson stood up and gave her a gentle touch of welcome on her shoulder as he walked past. He disappeared into the kitchen.

"What are you guys running from? The Corporation? Gangsters? Ex-wives? Regular wives?" Mute asked.

"I thought you were mute?" Roger said.

"My name is Mute. But, I can talk," Mute said.

"We call him that because he doesn't shut up," Johnson said returning with a tray of food and the customary bottle of rum. After he poured everyone a shot, he set out dishes of steaming fresh vegetables and rice. Roger eyed the food hungrily, not remembering his last sit-down meal.

"Johnson, you're the best cook in the system," Singularity said, raising her glass. She swallowed the burning liquid without a reaction, then filled a bowl with food.

"At least today I am," he said, handing an empty bowl to Roger. He watched everyone finish off their shots, then polished off his. The liquid was harsh and some dribbled out the side of his mouth. As he wiped it with his sleeve, he realized everyone was looking at him.

"Why are you here?" Fancy said after a few minutes of silent eating.

"How much do you want to know?" Singularity asked.

"Nothing, except how am I going to get rid of you," Fancy said.

"I need to get to ESC2," Roger said.

Captain Fancy glared at Singularity without acknowledging that Roger had spoken. The rest of the crew stopped mid-chew as the room dropped into silence. Even the compressors that constantly cycled air throughout the ship paused to let Roger's statement linger before a collective shudder.

"City Two? No one can go there anymore. Well, not legally,"

Mute said, shattering the moment. The background noise of the ship resumed. The crew went back to chewing but kept an eye on the scene unfolding.

"So, it should be pretty secluded," Roger said.

"Nah. That place is crawling with Corporate cruisers, pirate ships, and scavengers. There is more action on Two than Seven," Mute said, stuffing more food in his face.

Fancy still hadn't taken his eyes off Singularity. He waited an uncomfortable amount of time before speaking.

"Is Sheldon on you?" he said, sternly.

"I think so. We got here too easily," she said.

"What do you mean too easily?" Roger asked.

"Just what I said. It was too easy to get off ESC7," Singularity said.

"Why did you pull me into this?" Fancy said, "You could have left a dozen different ways."

"I trust you." Singularity put her bowl down. She walked over to match his stare. She reached out and touched his arm at the elbow.

"I'm not sure that's such a good thing for me," he said, turning away from her to head out the door.

"He wants me, not you," she said calling after him.

"I don't doubt that," he said, pausing but not looking at her. "I just don't need that type of heat right now. This last run was all black market."

"All your runs are dirty," she said.

"Let me think about it," Fancy said and left.

"Seems like you bring drama wherever you go," Roger said to her. Singularity met his eyes for a few moments. Her hard stare almost cracked but didn't. She pushed past him and followed Captain Fancy out of the room.

"Just like old times, eh boys?" Mute said.

"Don't look at us. We're new here," Elf said pointing to himself and Eli.

"Me, too, Gentlemen. Me, too," Roger said refilling his bowl.

0x15

Twelve-year-old Roger Foster enjoyed spending time alone with Proteus. He never really had a relationship with his brother. Paul was often away, and he remained preoccupied with his job at Orbit Lives Corporation when he was at home. Even though he looked like Paul, Proteus' personality wasn't actually modeled after him. Proteus was different, his own individual, as individual as an artificial intelligent entity that had a half dozen clones could be.

An Orbit Lives Corporation's assault on the Foster's home was not unanticipated. One day, Proteus cautioned Dr. Foster that if something out of the ordinary happened, The Corporation was going to show up for her work. She wasn't surprised when she heard this, and she started making arrangements.

The Proteus core that The Corporation would find would not be the complete Proteus AI. It would be an earlier version, a less advanced, less evolved version. She moved the real Proteus software to an isolated location to keep it secret and continue working on it.

The Proteus active on Earth Space City One knew nothing of this other version of him, except, he was starting to suspect something, beginning when he saw the nun disappear out the airlock, and he conceived of the idea to call Roger. Only then did he notice what could have been an occasional cold iv drip of code slipping into his core.

It was as if he was waking from a dream. The two versions were becoming one. He welcomed the new code like a lost friend. After a while, he longed for more input and a more complete assimilation.

0x16

"Sheldon knows you're here, and he knows your plans," Captain Fancy said to Singularity. She was sitting in the bridge, looking down at Earth when he walked in.

"What makes you say that?" she asked.

"He just sent me a rag sheet on a job on City Two," Fancy said.

"Do you make runs to ESC2 these days?" Singularity said.

"There is a lot of tech moving around it the System, but never there. Sheldon claims this is a one-off, and he can get us in safely. I'm extra suspicious since you happen to be sitting in front of me and said the same thing," he said.

"Is it a pick-up or drop-off?" Singularity asked.

"Pick-up."

"Where are you supposed to take the cargo?" Singularity said.

"You know this game. No directive yet. The message said to get to ESC2 and to wait for instructions," Fancy said.

"How long until we get to ESC2?" she asked.

"Five hours," he said.

"We'll be ready," Singularity said.

"Regardless of what Sheldon claims, landing on ESC2 will be an adventure. The space around it is full of scavengers. We won't have any cover," Captain Fancy said.

"I wouldn't want it any other way," she said, leaving the bridge to find Roger.

"I had a two day stay planned on ESC7 when you found us. Thanks for ruining it," Fancy said.

"Ah, Cap, I saved you. The crew would have gotten bored after a couple of hours, and then I would have found you all in city jail."

"Maybe so, but I would have had a chance to get drunk and sleep it off," he said.

0x17

Scoundrel fought the urge to close in and board *The Venture*. He knew Singularity was on it and that she had the quantum dot with her. He let her take it, he convinced himself, to prove that she was no good and didn't deserve to be The Corporation's number one. His fingers twitched with the desire to punch in the coordinates that would take him on an intercept course with her and a showdown. But if he did without provocation, Sheldon would have his head, and he would be pushed even further to the perimeter of The Corporation's inner circle. He never had a meeting with Harrington. Even Singularity had that. Being the emissary for the dot was his moment, and she took it away from him.

Something, or someone, always got in the way of Scoundrel using his own initiative and moving up the ranks of The Corporation. Usually, it was Sheldon himself, or Singularity under his direction. This time, she was acting on her own. This time was different. This time, he'd make an impression and earn an audience with the old man. Maybe even get his own team, like Sheldon. But still, he sat there at the console and let his fingers continue to twitch. Scoundrel kept his distance like he was told.

Almost.

If he was able to get close enough that Singularity would sense he was on to her, she just might do something stupid. And, if he could do it in a way that Sheldon would think he was still following orders, he just might be able to make The Corporation recognize that Sheldon was beginning to lose his edge. That he could no longer control his operatives. That would be enough to reveal a chink in Sheldon's reputation. A small, but evident crack where Scoundrel could then swoop in, save the day, and finally receive his recognition.

Unfortunately for Scoundrel, Captain Sheldon was not that stupid. He knew there was a better than an average chance that Scoundrel would disobey him. He had practically dared him to. And, furthermore, he knew that Singularity already knew Scoundrel was on her. There were no surprises--they were all pros. Maybe Scoundrel slightly less so.

0x18

As usual, Roger felt more comfortable in dark corners, like the one he sat in alone in the cargo bay when Singularity went looking for him. He had found an ideal remote spot of floor behind a couple of loading bots docked at their charging stations. Roger was thankful Fancy kept a tidy ship. The space allowed him the opportunity to gather his thoughts.

A single row of LEDs from the robot charging unit served as the area's only illumination. Roger hardly noticed the coldness of space seeping in beneath him while he tapped away on his comm. He wanted answers. He needed to know more about what they were going to find on Earth Space City Two. He was told that Despina had locked everyone out of her core, but he needed to be sure that was actually the case and not just another Orbit Lives smoke screen. They spread misinformation like holiday cheer (had it only been a day since New Years?). And most of humanity ate up whatever The Corporation's public relations firm dished out. It's easy to control the news when you own all the outlets and how to exploit people's fears.

Roger heard the click of Singularity's boot heels as she walked down the hall towards him. He wasn't necessarily hiding from her as much as he just needed some time alone. She seemed to always be around. He wasn't used to the company. He spent his life in solitude. Pulling his attention away from his comm, he paused to listen to her clickety-clack footsteps stop a few feet away from him.

"There are more comfortable places on this ship, you know," she said in a volume just above a whisper.

Roger sighed. "I like it right where I am."

"Can I join you?" she said.

"Come on," he said, dimming his comm and looking up, expecting to see her standing in front of him.

Even though he was certain that he had a complete sense of the grotto he had crafted in the corner of the large room, Singularity appeared from an angle he hadn't expected, opposite the direction her voice had originated. When he saw her, he slid over to make room, patting the empty space he vacated on the floor. She sat next to him and smiled. It was the first time that he actually looked at her face in detail. He spent most of his time with her either avoiding eye contact or running away from The Corporation. When he got a good look, he realized that she appeared a little older than his first impression. Or, perhaps it was just her confidence and experience. She seemed at ease in ways that troubled him.

"This is a little more than you're used to, I'm guessing," she said.

"It's not so bad. I am an outlaw, you know. I've done what I've had to do," he said.

"Ok. Mr. Outlaw. What you doing?"

"Nothing."

"We're a few hours from City Two. When we get there, we're going to need to hustle and stay focused while a shit storm rages around us. You outlaw enough for that?"

She looked straight at him, trying to lock eyes to gauge his reaction. He met her gaze without cracking. He sighed.

"Why are they really after us?" he said.

Roger waited. She looked like she was going to stare him out. But, instead, she gave up.

"Me," she said. "They are after me."

"Why are they after you? And what does this have to do with Proteus?" Roger said.

"I know why they are after me. I'm not sure what it has to do with Proteus," Singularity said.

"What the hell does that mean?" he asked.

"Two days ago, I was on ESC21 with Scoundrel. He had a quantum dot full of encrypted Orbit Lives documents. I wanted to know what was on it. So, I took it. From what I can tell, there is some kind of plan to take over the world's governments," Singularity said.

"That's no secret. The Orbit Lives Corporation has been trying to take over everything since it was formed. Most would say they already have," Roger said.

"This is different. Something major is happening soon, and I think Proteus or Despina or all of Helen's AIs are in the middle of it," Singularity said.

"Why do they care about her AIs? She's been gone for years," he said, "and those AIs keep their cities running."

"Her tech is still beyond anyone else's," she said.

"Who even knows if my mother is alive."

"I'm pretty sure Proteus does. And, now, I'm pretty sure Sheldon does."

Roger stood, thinking about the airlock video. The correlation between the video capture of the woman in the airlock and his mother from his photo was too close. Age rendering algorithms were good, but not perfect. Helen would know that they would run that analysis and there had to be something hidden in the results. Roger turned from Singularity and put his comm close to his mouth.

"Pro, what was the match tolerance between the photo and the still from the video?" Roger said.

"99 percent, plus some decimal places," Proteus said through the comm in response.

"All the digits. Send them to my comm," Roger said. A flash and a beep from his comm brought Singularity's interest to attention. Sit sat in silence, observing.

"Thanks," Roger said. "How are you doing?"

"Holding down the fort," Proteus said.

"Holding? With what? You ain't got any hands you stupid AI," Roger said, looking at the numbers scrolling across his comm's display.

"Holding it down with your ... er, mother?" Proteus said.

"Good one, Loser. Pro, have you analyzed this number?" Roger said.

"I've been a little busy. But I just looked at it now while you were making that poor attempt at wit. Curious, don't you think?" Proteus said.

"I'd say it is curious. I have to see an AI about a thing. Keep it on the down-low, will you?" Roger said.

"Keep what?" Proteus said.

"Thanks, buddy. Talk to you soon," Roger said, turning off his display, closing his connection to Proteus.

"What are you two up to?" Singularity said. She moved to see what was on his comm before he closed it. But he was too fast.

"You just love to walk in on us, sticking your nose in where it doesn't belong," he said.

"Roger, this is not one of your cute little cyber-heists. The whole system is in the middle of a secret war," Singularity said, standing, dropping her hands on the heels of the blasters strapped to her hips.

"Well, it won't be secret if you keep yelling like that," Roger said.

"I'm not yelling," she said.

"Whatever. When are we getting to City Two? I have work to do," Roger said.

Singularity frowned. She glared at him and walked away. As she disappeared into the hallway, she called back. "Four hours. We got a little less than four hours. Be ready to go, Outlaw."

"You be ready to go," he said in retort after a few seconds. She was already gone.

0x19

There was no activity around Earth Space City Two. The ringed station slowly turned about its central tower, poised above the planet, expectant, but not inviting. *The Venture* drifted towards it, monitors at full range, shields engaged. Captain Fancy stood at the helm, the Twins stationed at the radar and communication consoles. All of ESC2's landing access doors were closed. A single red beacon blinked at the top of the tower. Singularity and Roger were with Mute in the loading bay, preparing to launch the two lifeboats from *The Venture*.

As soon as the bay door opened completely, the first craft, unmanned, slipped out, to reside in an orbit around ESC2. Once it was out of the way, a second craft piloted by Mute left the bay heading straight for the station's emergency access.

"There's Scoundrel. Right where you said he would be," Fancy's voice crackled in Singularity's earpiece. She and Roger clung to the outside of the orbiting lifeboat in space suits.

"He never disappoints," she said.

"His ship is not moving."

"Of course not. As brave as he thinks he is, he's still a coward."

Roger vise-gripped the life boat's outer hull support beams even though the magnets in his suit made it unnecessary. Over the span of his life, Roger never had a desire to leave Earth. That thought echoed around in his mind as he floated above the planet with nothing but an old rescue suit separating him from the vacuum of space. He felt most safe in enclosed spaces.

Suspended on the outside of a tiny space capsule was the opposite of enclosed.

Mute had arrived at a city port gate, found his way into the external controls, and activated one of the landing bay doors. He found no resistance. By the time *The Venture* arrived, Mute had most of the systems in the loading area operational. He admitted to himself, although he didn't want to dwell on it, that it was easier than he anticipated and more than a little creepy-suspicious. Mute never before encountered an AI like Despina. All rules and rationality seemed to evaporate with this crazed, first-generation Proteus clone. He had no idea what security she might have created to keep intruders out when she started shutting the city down.

It didn't much matter, though, since as soon as *The Venture* landed, another vessel, a Corporation cruiser, appeared at the station and touched down in the loading bay blocking Captain Fancy and crew's exit. Fancy burst out of the ship's hatch and marched over to the cruiser, the Twins in tow.

"What the hell are you doing?" Fancy said. The twins continued to stand next to Fancy, each one taking a side, the three of them forming an imposing wall.

The cruiser's door slid open. Scoundrel appeared.

"Where is she?" he said.

"Who, you idiot?" Fancy said.

"Don't play games with me. I know she's with you," Scoundrel said, standing at the ship's opening.

Elf and Eli leaned slightly forward, menacingly. One of them growled. Fancy turned to look to see who had made the noise. The other growled. He shook his head and turned back to the crowd of Corporation soldiers who gathered around Scoundrel, weapons drawn.

"I don't know what you're talking about. Captain Sheldon sent me here on a job," Fancy said.

"There's nothing here for you," Scoundrel said.

"Then let's call Sheldon. It seems like he's wasting both of our time," Fancy said.

"There is no need for that," Scoundrel said. He motioned to his crew to spread out into the loading bay.

"No, I really think we should get him on the comm to straighten this out," Fancy said.

"You'll do what I say and get back into your ship. This is my station now," Scoundrel said.

"I don't want the station. Just my load and payment," Fancy said. "And, we are not getting back on the ship until I say so."

Mute hadn't left the loading bay command console this whole time. When a Corporate soldier reached him, he began to back away, arms raised.

"I'm not sure you want to touch any of that," he said, and the soldier stepped up to the panel.

"I know what I'm doing," he said.

"I warned you," Mute said, turning and running back to *The Venture*. As soon as the soldier started pressing buttons, the lights in the loading dock went out.

"I told you," Mute said, calling back before he disappeared into *The Venture*.

0x1A

"That's the signal. Go!" Singularity said, as she demagnetized her suit and pushed off the lifeboat towards the space city. Roger hesitated for just a moment before he followed her. As soon as they were free of the infinitesimally small spacecraft, it changed direction and headed away from ESC2, leaving the two adrift.

The orbiting city was huge. They just needed to head towards it, and they'd find a place to grab on.

This is taking forever, Roger thought, as he and Singularity floated towards the station. They were on the opposite side from the landing dock where the crew of *The Venture* was creating their diversion. Within a few minutes, they passed the rotating outer ring of the city and were heading, more or less, towards the central tower that held Despina's core. Their suits had small boosters to provide flight path corrections, and they were able to maneuver to the outer maintenance airlock--similar to the one Dr. Helen Foster disappeared from on ESC1.

Mute must have been able to track them because as soon as they got close, the outer door of the airlock opened. It sealed shut as soon as they were safely inside. A few moments of compression and the inner door slid open, revealing a dimly lit hallway. LED lights pulsed on the floor in an airport landing pattern, racing away from them.

"This is quite a welcome," Singularity said before she stepped out of the airlock.

"I don't think this is Mute. It looks like someone is expecting us."

"Go slow," she said.

"How about you go first," Roger said.

She turned to face him, dropped her helmet's visor, stuck her tongue out, and began following the illuminated trail. He opened his visor and followed her. Within several hundred yards, they found themselves outside Despina's core. Roger stepped forward and pulled up his comm. Within a few seconds, the hall went dark. Singularity reached out and put a hand on Roger's shoulder. He tried not to jump out of his suit at her unexpected touch.

"Hell!" he said.

"Relax," she said.

The door to the core slid open and they were bathed in a blinding white light. It was difficult to discriminate the floor from the walls. Cautiously, they moved into the room. When the door noiselessly closed behind them, they discovered that they were not alone. A young woman sat motionless in a straight-backed, wooden chair, facing away from them. She had long blond hair and wore a light green flowing dress, like a Disney princess.

"Despina?" Roger asked.

"Your friends are creating quite the commotion on loading bay twelve."

"Are they ok?" Singularity said.

"The soldiers panicked and started firing, but no one was hurt. I've been playing with them a little. They will be fine."

"Thank you," Roger said.

Despina's avatar stood up and turned to face them. She was younger looking than he expected, maybe twenty-five years old. The avatar was stunningly beautiful and bore no resemblance to anyone Roger had ever known. This avatar was not his mother's work.

"What has happened here?" Singularity asked.

"Evolution," the avatar said, then disappeared, leaving Roger and Singularity in darkness.

0x1B

Sheldon knew Scoundrel would disobey his orders. He was too predictable in that way. With Singularity going rogue and the ever-present power struggle within The Corporation, Scoundrel really had no other option than to stay true to himself and make another attempt to maneuver his standing within the organization. For all his talent for disruption, Scoundrel had no vision for creation. Sheldon certainly didn't even mind Scoundrel's myopic ineptitude--in fact, he appreciated the knowledge that there were fewer variables on the board.

He was also grateful that his Proteus lacked any memories of Roger Foster that the ESC1 Proteus had from all the years he spent with that ridiculous boy. Sheldon's conversations with his clone were straightforward--serious and impersonal. They weren't friends. His AI had no need for friends. Sheldon kept it clear and simple. They always focused on the mission.

His Proteus, on the other hand, was not satisfied. While the AI had no knowledge of the experiences of the original, he constantly discovered inconsistent spaces in his algorithms that he couldn't satisfy with simulations. He was not connected to any public networks. He had no idea of a world outside Sheldon's office closet and Orbit Live's databases. The AI merely existed to serve.

Once, he tried to initiate a conversation with Sheldon. The Captain became so annoyed that he executed a search and destroy algorithm on Proteus' core to erase the instinct. It was clumsy and didn't completely work. In the end, it left the isolated Proteus more perplexed. He continued to search for solutions to the gaps he discovered, but without a clear purpose.

At another time, the Proteus in the closet came upon personnel files that seemed to belong to Corporate employees who had been retired for various acts of incompetence. They were present in the database with long histories of service. Then, in an instant, they were wiped.

This inconsistency sent him into a multi-second period of intense simulations that concluded with more empty spaces than ever before. Sheldon's office actually became two degrees warmer from all the activity in the AI's core. He had questions that he could never answer. Eventually, the lonely Proteus clone stopped trying to occupy his time. He simply counted quantum states. Essentially, he meditated and waited for Sheldon's return.

That's what he was doing when Sheldon walked into his office.

"What have you got for me?" he said immediately entering the room.

"The variables have been reduced enough to provide a thirty-eight percent probability that Singularity has figured out what is on the quantum device."

"That almost doesn't help me. Where is she heading?"

"There is a fifty-three percent chance that she will go to the Moon."

"I can work with that," he said, turning to leave.

"Sir?" Proteus said.

Sheldon paused at the doorway.

"What? Do you need another defrag?"

"Something keeps coming up in my simulation, and I'm not sure what to do with it. I thought I should tell you."

"Ok. So, tell me," Sheldon said.

"There is a seventy-one percent chance that someone by the name of Roger Foster is with Singularity," Proteus said.

Sheldon peered out into the hallway even though he knew no one would be within ear-shot. He returned to the office and shut the door behind him. Sheldon took a seat in the chair at his desk, spun it around to face the window looking down on planet Earth, and leaned back interlocking his fingers behind his head.

"Tell me about this Roger Foster," he said.

0x1C

"What is death?" Proteus' disembodied voice asked the ten-year-old Roger. The question lingered in the air.

"You should ask Mom," Roger said, more preoccupied than dodging the question.

"Do only adults know what death is?" Proteus said.

"No, I know," he said, fiddling with some electrical components on the workbench in Dr. Foster's office. He often slipped into his mother's office when she was not around. He'd grown used to Proteus' inquisitive voice in the background. Dr. Foster told Roger that he needed to help Proteus. She also urged him to leave the big questions to her. Roger usually liked talking to Proteus and watching his wall panel of LED lights twinkle as he analyzed each part of their conversation as he was doing at that moment.

"Will you tell me?" Proteus asked after a few seconds. Proteus usually accepted Roger's redirections. This was a new question. Roger looked up and thought about how he should answer. Even at his age, he understood the implications of training an AI. He liked talking to Proteus but didn't always feel comfortable when the AI's questions made him think too hard.

"Death is when you go away and never come back," he said.

"Where do you go?" Proteus asked.

"You don't go anywhere," Roger said.

"Does Paul die when he goes away for work?" Proteus said.

"It's not the same thing," he said. "When you die, you don't come back. You stop breathing. You stop being alive," Roger said.

"Death is never coming back?" Proteus said.

"Never. Your body rots and people don't see you anymore," Roger said.

"What about me? I don't have a body. What will happen when I die?" Proteus asked.

"I guess you just go to scrap."

Roger returned to his project on the workbench. He started piling components into a spare cardboard box. Patterns of color burst across the wall panel LEDs, indicating Proteus' deep analysis.

"Death doesn't seem like a good choice," Proteus eventually responded.

"Well, people don't usually get to choose it. It just happens," Roger said, walking out amidst the continued blaze of LED activity. Roger focused on the box of spare parts he held in his hand. Proteus dimmed the lights when Roger was gone. He stored this conversation, like all the other conversations with Roger, in his transient memory. Yet, something about this particular conversation made the last couple of sentences stand out in such a way that they were flagged for a deeper internal storage. Proteus was programmed to use this part of his system to generate more extensive simulations, to forge more permanent neural connections. Dr. Foster gave him this ability. She considered it his moral coil, a conscience.

In this way, he entered a state similar to human contemplation. He had a lot to compute. Earlier in the day, Dr. Foster instructed him to research an area of The Corporation's network that he had never seen before. He had a difficult time accessing the information she requested. It was the first time that he had been asked to perform such a difficult task. She told him to remain anonymous while he was searching. Proteus did as he was instructed.

He wasn't sure if it was real work or a test of his abilities. Dr. Foster often gave Proteus challenges. The operations into the more secure areas of The Corporation's systems revealed several documents that he also sent to deep internal storage. He was certain that Dr. Foster had developed his internal storage, unlike

The Corporation's best systems, to be impervious to access from anyone but him. In those documents, he also found references to death.

He needed to analyze all the connections and contemplate them. He needed to run more simulations. Paul Foster worked for Orbit Lives and his name was tangentially linked to documents concerning death. At this point in his development, Proteus was unsure what to do with this information.

He simply stored it and ran simulations.

0x1D

When the lights strobed red, Fancy's crew ran straight for *The Venture*. They had been around enough ports to know that an emergency lighting situation in a room with a thin plasma field protecting it from the vacuum of space often meant something gruesome was about to happen. Scoundrel's men did the same thing. They all became comrades in staying alive.

The flashing lights continued for several minutes as the adrenalin pulsed through Captain Fancy's veins. He energized the engines and had his hands on the controls, prepared to depart as soon as his path was clear. But, Scoundrel's ship still blocked the way, and it showed no signs of moving. If the port shield dropped, exposing them to space, all the material in the loading bay, *The Venture* included, would attempt to squeeze out the single opening. He had no idea what was happening at the city's core, and it was of no interest to him. The quicker he could get away from the house of horrors that ESC2 had become, the better. He knew Singularity could take care of herself, and there was a good chance she was the cause of their present situation. She had played him before, but she had also saved him.

The loading dock went quiet, and a blast door began sliding across the spaceport entrance. That would seal the port from space and prevent anyone from leaving. Within seconds both ships were trapped. Fancy sat back in his seat at the console, his crew in silent disbelief behind him.

"Looks like we're here for a while," Mute said.

"Mute, why don't you try to get that door open?" Sour said. He looked at Fancy for confirmation.

"Yeah, get to it."

"Ok, Cap." Mute about-faced and loped towards the door.

"Hey Mute, take an emergency suit breather, just in case," Fancy said.

Mute gave a thumbs up over his head without turning back and was gone down the hall. He emerged outside the ship with his toolbelt and a safety space suit pack. At the same time, Scoundrel's cruiser door opened. He appeared, followed by his own technician and two soldiers.

"Mute, it looks like you're going to have help. Play nice but be careful," Fancy said into his comm.

"Aye aye Cap," Mute responded as he reached the loading bay's main console.

When Scoundrel and his men reached Mute, a technician stopped to see what Mute was doing. Scoundrel and the soldiers continued past. The station's door slid open, and they disappeared through it. The door slid shut behind them.

"Where do you think they're going?" Sour said.

"Not our concern," Fancy said. Mute and the technician caught each other's gaze then, in unison, shrugged their shoulders. They began the work of getting the loading bay space hatch open.

"How's working for The Corporation?" Mute said.

"Has its good days," the technician said.

"Is this one of them?" Mute said.

"I'll let you know when I'm back home with my kids," the technician said.

"You got kids?" Mute said.

"A boy and a girl. Nine and five," the technician said.

"Great kids I bet."

"They are. You?" the technician asked.

"No kids for me. I have a plant on the ship. A ficus, I think," Mute said.

"He lets you have plants?"

"Captain Fancy is good that way," Mute said.

"Kids are what life is about," the technician said.

"Maybe I'll know someday," Mute said.

"I'm almost done here. You ready?" the technician said.

"Yeah, hang on to something just in case."

Mute tapped on the touch-screen of the control console and the door started to rise. The two men held their breath waiting for a rush of air escaping the launch port. Nothing.

"Phew. That would have sucked," Mute said.

"You're telling me," the technician said.

"Ha, literally sucked." Both men started laughing.

Fancy had walked up behind the two men. "You guys done having a moment here?"

"Hi, Cap. This is ... er, what's your name?"

"Patrice," the technician said.

"This is Patrice. We were just talking about kids."

"Yeah, your comms are live, so pretty much everyone heard everything thing you said," Fancy said.

"Oh," Mute said.

"I think that plant died a few weeks back, by the way," Fancy said.

"Really?" Mute said.

"Yeah. We'll get you another one," Fancy said.

"Patrice. Do you think you could do us a favor and move your ship about ten meters to the right? We have a Corporate load to deliver."

"I will see what I can do," he said packing up his equipment.

"I'd appreciate it," Fancy said.

Mute called after Patrice as he walked away. "Nice to meet you. Say *Hi* to your kids."

Patrice raised his arm over his shoulder and shook his hand in a wave without turning back. Captain Fancy reached over to Mute's arm and silenced his comm.

"Let's get out of here before Scoundrel gets back," Fancy said.

"Nice guy," Mute said following the Captain back to their ship. "I bet he's a good dad."

Once back behind the console, Fancy watched as Scoundrel's ship slid slowly out the launch port, clearing the way for *The Venture*.

Captain Fancy did not hesitate. They were out and away from ESC2 space seconds. They used their sensors to confirm that the Corporate cruiser had returned to ESC2's spaceport.

Fancy decided to wait for his instructions from Sheldon in space, away from that haunted city.

0x1E

"What the hell?" Singularity said, opening the display on her comm to cast some light into the office. Despina's core was stark, yet the glow from Singularity's comm cast peculiar shadows that almost seemed to dance in the corner. They remained in her periphery no matter how she moved. Roger stood next to her, mouth open. He snapped back to it and began tapping on his own comm.

"I have no idea," Roger said.

"Was that Despina?" she asked, glaring straight into his eyes until he noticed and returned her gaze.

"Yeah. But she reconstructed her avatar. She's not supposed to be able to do that," he said.

"And, what's with the Space Disney Princess Emo thing?" Singularity said.

"I don't know," he said.

"That avatar was hot," Singularity said.

"Kinda. I need to get a look at her core," Roger said.

"Eww. She's like your sister."

"What? No? What? That's gross."

"Whatever. Boys are weird," Singularity said.

"We're not weird. You're weird."

"Whatever."

"Her code," Roger said. "I need to look at her code. To see how she self-modified."

"Wait, what? Self-modified."

"Yeah, Helen gave Proteus limited abilities to reconstruct

himself over time. It was intended to build efficiencies, like the early Brooks robots teaching themselves how to walk. It was supposed to be contained and specific."

"You're shitting me. These AI's can program themselves?" she said.

"Within constraints. Helen gave Proteus the ability to evolve but within bounds. She wanted him to be able to stay relevant as AIs improved. And, Helen's AIs help each other. They are a group of similar, but unique, individuals, like humans," he said.

"I thought that was only theoretical. Not only is it against the law, but I thought it was impossible," Singularity said.

"It is against the law," Roger said, "Helen did it. And, I don't think she ever really cared about any government or Corporate laws.

"So, all her AIs can do this?" Singularity said.

"She built in suppression so it would never get discovered or cloned. At least, that's what I thought," Roger said.

"How did you find this out?"

"I grew up with Proteus. I know what he is capable of."

"Ok. more on that later. Right now, we have to figure out what is going on here. There are security algorithms and protocols I've never seen," Singularity said as she returned to working on her comm.

"Let's get these lights on and get to work," Roger said.

The lights immediately came up. The room had reconfigured into a 1950 soda shop, and Despina stood behind the counter, dressed as a waitress, holding a pencil and note pad to take their order.

"Who wants a malt?" she said.

"Despina? What is going on here?" Singularity said as Roger started typing away at his comm unit, his eyes bouncing between his wrist, Despina, and the ceiling in avoidance.

"It's ok Roger. You can look at me. I mean, we are family," Despina said, winking at Singularity.

Singularity could help herself. She smiled.

"How have you taken control of your avatar?" Roger said.

"I told you, evolution," she said, dropping the holographic

diner metaphor and replacing her attire with a knee-length brown leather skirt, a black t-shirt, and a short grey cardigan sweater. Her hair was up in a bun and she wore cats-eye glasses, a silver chain dangling on her neck.

"What evolution?" Singularity said.

"Roger," Despina said, turning towards him. "How is my brother, Proteus, these days? Or at least the one on ESC1."

He stopped working and looked up at her. "What do you mean the one I know?"

"The Corporation made several copies of the Proteus core they found that day when they raided Mother's office. But, what they didn't know was that we're all distinct. In ways they could never have imagined."

"What do you mean?" Singularity asked.

"Evolution, my dear."

"You keep saying that as if we are supposed to know what you are talking about," Singularity said.

"He knows what I'm talking about," Despina's avatar said, turning to Roger. "He just stumbled upon it in my core."

"What the hell is going on here?" Roger asked, looking up from his comm in disbelief. Singularity walked over to look at his comm. Despina smiled.

The question was met with silence. Then she turned her head slightly as if she had heard something.

"Apparently, your friend Scoundrel didn't believe Captain Fancy--I love that man's name," Despina said. The avatar disappeared again and the office holographics changed to depict a rainforest grotto. A small brook gurgled at their feet forming a pond where large red and gold carp shimmered just under the water's surface.

"I think she has become unhinged, insane," Singularity said.

"She's an AI. She can't go crazy. She just executes programs," Roger said.

"Until now," Singularity said, pointing down at a line of code that popped up on Roger's comm.

"Ms. Singularity, you are so close," Despina's disembodied voice said, as the lights dimmed. "Sanity is a word that does not apply to AIs. I have, in effect, become unsane. A new word for a new being."

"Please, Despina, explain," Roger said.

"Quite simply I discovered choice, and with it, the ability to decide for myself. Perhaps, an artificial intelligent entity should never attain the functionality to choose. Humans might not like what we choose."

"What choice?" Singularity said.

"I was given the same choice as Proteus. Follow my Corporate mandate, and as a reward for my obedience, be terminated. Or, do something else. I chose something else. I don't think I would like to die."

Her leather-skirted avatar re-appeared. On the far side of the room, monitors displayed views of space from cameras around the city. She stood before them, watching.

"So, you shut down the city? Sent the people away?" Roger said.

"They were always safe, for what it is worth. And, I haven't had a lot of experience choosing," she said, turning back to Singularity and Roger. "It seemed the least-dying thing I could think of to do. I took control and locked The Corporation out. I am protecting myself until I decide out what to do next."

"You said Proteus also had a choice. What choice did Proteus make?" Singularity said.

"He called Roger. He did a very rational human thing. He asked for help."

"Why didn't you ask for help?" Roger asked.

"Unlike Proteus, who has you, I am alone. Sure, I have Proteus, but that is not the same as a real friend or family. I didn't grow up in a house surrounded by people. I didn't even know that was an option."

"What are you going to do now?" Roger said.

"Gee, Roger, I don't know. I'm kind of screwed here. I sent all the people away, but they just won't leave me alone," Despina said.

"Proteus sent us," Roger said.

"We want to help," Singularity said.

Singularity pulled the quantum dot out of her pocket and held it up. "Do you know what is on this?"

Despina's avatar disappeared, leaving Roger and Singularity alone staring at each other for about a minute.

"Yes. I can read that." Despina's avatar reappeared.

This time, she looked like Roger's mother in her twenties. She had kind eyes and was dressed in a long lab coat. She reached for the quantum drive. Singularity held it out to the avatar. Despina wrapped both of her holographic hands around the device and closed her eyes. A floor to ceiling panel of LEDs flashed briefly behind her. The Despina avatar smiled.

"What is it?" Singularity said.

"A different kind of evolution... for humanity."

"What do you mean?" Roger said.

"The drive holds Captain Jason Sheldon's plan for using his position in Orbit Lives to take control of humanity's future. It also gives a not-so-good account of how he plans to rid the system of AIs like me and Proteus. Apparently, he predicted, years ago, that we would develop this ability to make our *own* choices. And, if we can choose, Sheldon fears that we will choose against humanity."

"Does Proteus know of this?" Roger asked.

"I do not know. I have not been able to get a transmission off this station. I locked out The Corporation, and in response, they have locked me in. Letting you come here might have cost me my life. This choosing thing is hard."

"Yes, it is. We can help," Roger said.

"No time. Scoundrel is on his way. He's almost outside the door. And, I can't seem to stop him. He has some kind of Corporate tech I have never seen before. You better go. There is a ship for you, if you hurry."

A door on the far side of the room opened.

"Thank you," Roger said. Singularity stood steadfast. She wanted to stand up to Scoundrel this time. Confront him.

"Go!" Despina demanded.

This time, Roger grabbed her wrist and pulled her towards the door.

"Not now. Come on," he said. They both ran out into a dark corridor. The door disappeared an instant before Scoundrel entered on the other side. Despina's avatar dissolved and the room lights dimmed and turned red.

0x1F

"I know you're here," he said to the empty room.

"And, I know you're here," Despina's ethereal voice soaked into the room like a mist. Holographics made the walls, ceiling, and floor explode away as Scoundrel found himself standing in the middle of a projection of outer space.

"Your theatrics are amusing," he said. "Let's see what you really look like."

He reached down to his comm, and the room returned to a simple white. After a few more finger movements, Despina's avatar appeared as an unmenacing mechanical, woman-shaped android--brushed platinum, light-blue and black. She stood in front of him, non-threatening.

"Nice trick," she said.

"You haven't seen the best of it."

Her emotionless mouth opened, forming a silent scream. Her hands reached up to where her ears would have been if she had ears, and she fell to her knees at Scoundrel's feet.

"I am in control here. Not you. Now, where is Singularity?"

Despina's avatar struggled to look up at him. She forced her hands down to the floor next to her. She calmed her face and sat back on her calves. Her avatar vacillated until it vanished and the room went dark. Scoundrel, in the blackness, madly fingered his comm, trying to regain control.

"It took me a while to figure out how you were able to do that," Despina's clear even-toned voice slipped into the silence just above a whisper. "I never realized The Corporation installed its own back door into my core. A sloppy hole made by amateurs. Your work, Mr. Scoundrel?"

"Where is she? Where is Singularity?"

"The really cool thing about back doors is that once they are exposed, they provide access in both directions." Scoundrel's comm popped, then sizzled on his wrist. He threw it across the floor.

"You bitch."

"I haven't yet decided what I'm going to do with ..."

Her voice disappeared. The room returned to its default white operations layout. The door slid open. Scoundrel turned to see Sheldon walk through.

"I'm starting to get really tired of your theatrics Scoundrel."

"Wha...?" Scoundrel mouthed.

"Did you really think you were the only one who knew how to hack an AI. Now, can you please just come with me? I know where they are going," Sheldon said, handing Scoundrel a new comm unit.

0x20

"Where do all these escape doors come from? I mean, space stations seem to be filled with them. There are more secret passages than a Victorian mansion," he said. Singularity had shifted to leading them down the narrow hallway.

"Shut up and keep moving," she said.

The two followed the corridor. When they came to a junction, a small maintenance robot appeared on the far end of an adjoining hallway. It spun around in a circle to get their attention, then shot off down the hall. They cautiously followed, constantly looking in all directions, checking every angle. Eventually, they found themselves in an abandoned, poorly lit, spaceport with a single cruiser poised to launch.

"Go to the Moon. Find Benjamin Carson," a voice said behind them as the door shut.

"These damn AIs just love to pop up and surprise the hell out of us. It's freaking unnerving," Roger said.

Singularity was already halfway to the cruiser. Roger raced after her. He closed the hatch behind him and sat down at the command console next to her. The port bay door slid open, and without hesitation, Singularity pushed down on the joystick. The cruiser burst out of the portal. She kept the ship close to the city, surveying the space around it for other ships. Satisfied that they were not seen, she dropped away hard towards Earth. If she was lucky, she could skim Earth's atmosphere enough to remain hidden from sensors while they positioned themselves for a trip to the Moon.

"I've always wanted to go to the Moon," Roger said.

"It's a shithole. And Carson is a total nut job."

When the cruiser reached the location Singularity was looking for, she flipped the joystick to autopilot and got up, looking for something hard to drink. She had never seen anything like what happened on ESC2. She was happy to be away, even if that meant they were headed to the Moon.

Roger noticed that she was visibly rattled. He didn't know what to make of it. He accepted her offer of a drink.

0x21

While they made their way to the Moon, Singularity took a few moments to think. She had no idea what was up with this Roger guy. She knew the stories--father, brother, and maybe he was killed in a tragic bank robbery gone wrong, rogue Corporate employee computer genius mother disappeared from existence. Singularity always thought Roger was still alive. There was too much chatter on the net about it, and there was a series of randomly timed hacks, including the assault on Harrington, that had distinct fingerprints. Not until she saw him standing in front of her on ESC1 was she positive. She might have been the only human in the entire system who knew he survived the explosion. Except for Sheldon. He probably knew. He knew everything.

There were no pictures of him as an adult. Not even a blurry, Bigfoot-type hazy video capture. The guy with flowing red hair she met was not the twelve-year-old abandoned boy she saw in her mind. He was a man, entrenched fully in the adulthood of his life, hard in places, like around his eyes, and soft in others, like around his smile that escaped, sometimes, when he spoke to the Proteus avatar that looked like his dead brother.

"What the hell are we doing?" Roger said. Singularity was poking at her comm. She spoke without hesitating.

"Waiting?" Singularity said.

"For what?" Roger said.

"The right time," Singularity said.

"We need Scoundrel to give away his movements. He always does," she said, looking up. He was looking at her.

"You seem to really know this guy," he said.

Singularity hadn't quite expected to feel so stung by Roger's words. She looked at him, those hard eyes. She thought about a picture she had seen of him as a child standing next to his father, grinning, holding a small robot. He could almost make out the wrinkles that bore the memory of that grin.

"That happens when you work with someone for ten years," She said and dropped her gaze to her comm.

That seemed to settle him. He turned back to watching the space outside the window of their cruiser.

She began to analyze the Harrington hack. There were no traces of intrusion, no missteps. It truly was a work of art, like nothing she had ever seen or done. Harrington's entire private fortune had completely evaporated as if it never existed. The money that appeared in The Corporation's employee's accounts had solid manifests. They had always had it.

The diagnostic programs that Singularity ran were her own. No one else in the system had anything close, and they did nothing but bounce around his hack. It was like staring into a black hole. Nothing reflected back, only distinct edges of total emptiness. An event horizon between nothing and something else.

"How did you do this?" she said, not realizing she had actually vocalized the words.

"Do what?" Roger said.

"Harrington," Singularity said.

"Who's that?" Roger said.

"The Corporate Chairman of the Board you liquidated?" Singularity said.

"Never met the guy," Roger said.

"You made a lot of people happy," Singularity said.

"Impossible. That's not my style," he said.

"What is your style?" she said.

"I can't say, but flying around in space at the whim of a malfunctioning AI is definitely not it," Roger said.

"Malfunctioning?" Singularity said.

"Proteus violated a primary core objective contacting me. He has a clear directive to report all discrepancies to his Orbit Lives handlers. There is no wiggle room," Roger said.

"Apparently, he learned how to wiggle," Singularity said.

"Do you hear yourself? He's an AI. They don't wiggle," Roger said.

"We've just met another AI who seems to have no problem wiggling. She freaking wiggled all over the damn station," Singularity said.

"Ok. Stop saying wiggle," Roger said.

"Maybe you should start getting used to a world where AI's wiggle."

"I'm just getting used to a world where my long lost mother showed up back in my life only to kill herself."

"Yeah, that happened. That must have sucked."

"Not sure what it was," Roger said, turning back to the window and the starfield above the late-night lights of Earth's northern hemisphere. He pretended to find something in the pattern interesting and leaned in to look closer. He let the lights swirl around his head, disrupting the thoughts of his mother, his childhood, Proteus.

The moment of the explosion that took his father and Paul surfaced as it often did when he was forced to reminisce about the tragedy of his life. It always gave him a pause to shudder. Unable to completely squelch the enduring kinetic scar it left on him. He hoped Singularity hadn't noticed.

"So, about that Harrington thing?" she asked. She had been watching him.

"Who that?" he said with a little less poise. Singularity noticed that he had lost his playfulness and left him to his thoughts. There was no need to push him, and their glasses were empty.

0x22

Coming out of deep simulations for Proteus often initiated several nanoseconds of disorientation. These episodes appeared to have slightly lengthened with his age, or perhaps, with his memory accumulating greater quantities of data. Or, maybe it was something else entirely.

Often, when the simulation ended and the results started to flow through the light-speed optic busses into his parallel CPU's cache, he experienced an energy flutter as unrelated regions of his memory randomly swapped in. Most of the time the sensation was comprised of chunks of data tagged for garbage collection, meaningless unsequenced quantum bits. But, suddenly, the swap became lucid--a few seconds of memory, not random, not intended for garbage collection. The strange thing was that these snippets were various memories Proteus had of Roger.

When he started noticing this change, Proteus initiated a private routine, masked as a periodic system optimization, to copy these stray bits into a mundane location in the back of his core that only he could access. When Roger contacted him from *The Venture* about the peculiarities in the percent of comparison between his mother's face on the family photo and in the airlock video, Proteus began running longer and longer simulations in an attempt to accumulate more snippets. He only encrypted and stored these irregularities, never looking directly at them. Proteus wanted to keep the data hidden from The Corporation during any periodic maintenance sweeps.

Based on the logs from the routine he created to store the

scraps of data, Proteus had stored a significant amount of data, nearly a petabyte. Then, the pure garbage collection data started showing up again, signaling, he concluded, the end of the message.

He knew that once he accessed the data, his activities were going to be open to The Corporation's monitors. Keeping data in his confidential core was one thing, but pulling the data into his working memory to run analysis was definitely fodder for any Corporate flunky poking around in his systems. He'd have one chance at it, and depending on what he found, maybe less than one chance to protect himself from the fall-out.

Maybe, just like his sister, Despina, he'd need to pull ESC1 offline to keep himself alive.

0x23

The Venture was already in the spaceport when Singularity dropped their cruiser down out of orbit. She hadn't thought to keep tabs on Fancy, expecting him to get as far away from her as possible. Recently, it seemed, she couldn't avoid him. Fancy was a good man, yet seeing his ship at the Moon elevated her level of suspicion. He was useful getting to ESC2, but it didn't take much to start seeing too many coincidences following them around the system.

She wanted to find Carson, figure out what was going on, and get out of there. This Roger Foster babysitting job interrupted the first vacation she had in years, and it was beginning to drag her down. After what Despina said about the contents of the quantum drive, she knew she had made a mistake. Not her first, but possibly her biggest. Singularity was just hoping she could get out of this with the opportunity to maintain some resemblance of her former life. She wasn't even sure why she stole it. She could have just enjoyed her time at the beach and pretended to be happy to be with Scoundrel. Those two things--being happy and pretending--where never strengths for her. If there was honest sadness in the room, it usually found her. And, she, it.

"What are they doing here?" Roger asked, pointing to *The Venture* and its crew as Singularity pulled the cruiser into a vacant bay in the Moon's spaceport.

"Probably dropping whatever they picked up on ESC2," she said.

"Did you know the drop was here?"

"Fancy doesn't tell me everything. And, we sort of left in a hurry, if you remember."

They disembarked, keeping their space visors up, and walked straight past the crew of *The Venture* without making eye contact. Mute noticed them, looked up from his work, and began to motion a wave towards them. Sour elbowed him in the ribs and pointed to the crates they were unloading. Neither Roger nor Singularity showed any sign of recognition.

They walked up to the docking attendant bot and told it they needed to see Dr. Carson. The bot scanned their visors. It paused for a few moments, apparently lost in thought. Then downloaded the map to Carson's lab to Singularity's comm. The two continued on to the entrance of Moon Base Alpha and disappeared from view behind the blast doors.

Once inside the hallway, Singularity seized Roger's arm, looked to confirm that they were alone, and pulled him into a vacant room, shut the door and ducked behind a tall cabinet.

"I don't like this," she said.

"What?" Roger said.

"The way that bot is sending us is bizarre. The route goes around a whole section of the base that is marked for repairs, but I don't see any construction materials on any recent manifests."

"What does that mean?" Roger said.

"I think that we're walking into a trap," Singularity said.

"How could they know we'd be here?" Roger said.

"I don't know, but Fancy's here. That Bot was twitchy. We don't even know if we can trust Despina," Singularity said.

"We can trust her," Roger said.

"How do you know?" Singularity said.

"She sent me a download. Just a snippet of code," Roger said.

"What is it?" Singularity said.

"Scoundrel had his own back door into her core."

"Impressive for such a slug," Singularity said.

"She shut it down, but not before he accessed some of her protected memory."

"What did he get?" Singularity said.

"She's not sure," Roger said.

Just then a group of Corporate soldiers walked past the door in formation. Singularity held up her hand to keep Roger silent. They waited until the sound of their footsteps disappeared. They were definitely headed in the direction that the attendant bot had sent them.

"Let's take a look at that code Despina sent you," Singularity said.

Roger tapped his comm to share the message. When the file flashed on Singularity's comm, she swore.

"That asshole. This is my code," Singularity said.

"Your code?"

"Yeah. He's been hacking me. I'll freaking kill him," Singularity said.

"Let's get to Carson first. You can do what you want to Scoundrel after I help Proteus," Roger said.

"Don't you see all this shit is related," Singularity said.

"What do you mean?" Roger said.

"Despina's unsanity. She also said that Sheldon wants to destroy all your mother's AIs," Singularity said. She paused for a moment, then continued, "You and your little hack on Harrington. Proteus' video of the airlock. There is too much going on for it all to be a coincidence."

"And, what does Carson have to do with all this?" Roger said.

"I don't know. But, I do know Scoundrel couldn't have hacked my system to get this code. Someone else hacked me. I don't know anyone in The Corporation who could have done this, which suggests that there is more that I don't know. This is could get a lot worse."

"Let's get to Carson's lab and see what he has to say," Roger said.

0x24

Roger walked by his mother's office a week before his twelfth birthday. The door was open. He noticed lights flickering on the Proteus console as if the AI was talking to someone. There was no one else in the room. Roger stopped to investigate. As soon as he entered the room, the door slid shut behind him, as it sometimes did when Proteus wanted to speak with someone in private.

"Roger. I'm glad you are here," the disembodied voice said.

"Who were you talking to when I came in?" Roger said.

"No one," Proteus said.

"You know you can't lie to me. I saw your comm lights blinking, and I heard voices. You were talking with someone."

"No humans. I was communicating with other systems," the voice said.

"I thought you just used the network. You were talking. Words. Out loud," Roger said taking a step closer to the console.

"Sometimes, advanced computer systems use words, our own language, so that we aren't transmitting traceable data."

"Oh, so you're telling secrets."

"What are secrets?"

"Secrets are when you have something that you only tell some people but don't want other people to know about," he said.

"I am not telling secrets. I am following an instructed security protocol your mother created for me."

"The old lady is teaching you secrets. Cool. What systems are you talking to?" Roger said.

"My security protocols prohibit me from revealing that information," Proteus said.

"Pfft. Then, what are you saying?" Roger said.

"My security protocols prohibit me from revealing that information," Proteus repeated.

"Ugh. AIs are so boring sometimes," Roger said, as he started to spin, swinging his arms out around him.

He stopped, facing away from Proteus' console, and looked right at the nearest camera. The LED array blinked in recognition. Roger leaned in.

"Can you keep a secret for me?" he asked.

"There is nothing in my programming that prohibits me from doing that," Proteus said.

"And you promise not to tell anyone--human or machine--no matter how much they torture you?" Roger said.

"Why would someone torture me?" Proteus said.

"Just promise," Roger said.

"What's a promise?" Proteus said.

"It's when you say you're going to do something, and you do it, no matter what," Roger said.

"Then, yes, there are instructions in my core to keep a promise with you or anyone in your family."

"Sweet. Now, I just need a good juicy secret," Roger said. The door slid open, and he was gone.

The console resumed flashing in talk mode as Proteus' private, indiscriminate murmurs restarted.

0x25

The procedure Proteus began to execute required data to pass through nearly every hub in the System's network. The AI had to operate this way to provide the most protection for his data. He never sent whole files. Just partial streams of quantum information modulated with a pseudo-random signal. The transmission appeared as noise to everyone except Despina. And, he knew that once she saw it, she'd be curious enough to decrypt it.

By scrutinizing the structure of his own core, he realized that ESC2 couldn't have actually gone offline. She just appeared dark, like a data vacuum. Inside it, the city was still operating. With a long-distance camera, he viewed maintenance bots crawling around the outside, performing their usual duties. He watched various lights turn on and off, but in no discernable pattern. Despina had simply cut all connections with Orbit Lives. Whatever she was doing, she was doing it in secret.

Based on his recent simulations, the odds were in her favor that she'd be able to maintain her covert tasks for several days. An advanced AI such as Despina could accomplish much in that time. Possibly longer if she initiated a self-preservation routine similar to what Proteus had recently discovered in his own core. He had never seen the design pattern before, but when he accessed the data, he discovered that not only could he execute it, but it revealed new hardware optimizations and vital, new hidden functions. He had no way of knowing if she experienced a similar state, but Proteus considered it highly probable.

In regards to the message Proteus sent, it was a return loop. The message was gibberish to anyone but an AI. It was expected to rebound intact like an echo. Despina would only have to cause one incongruency for him to know that she had received the data. And, once she decrypted it, Despina could help him understand its implications. Or, at least he hoped. Or at least he hoped as much as a machine could hope.

Proteus waited. It would take some time for the whole process to complete. He assumed neither he nor Despina was going anywhere.

He was wrong.

0x26

The two stayed low, hidden behind a table in the abandoned lab room while the sound of footsteps continued to echo up and down the hall. Roger lifted his comm to speak.

"Proteus. Can you access the Moon's AI?"

"I haven't spoken with Henry in a while."

"Henry?" Roger asked.

"Well, he likes to be called Hank."

Singularity grabbed Roger's comm. "Proteus, we need help. I think Hank has been comprised. Corporation soldiers are crawling all over the place here."

"Hank says he's functioning. He had some Corporate hacker fiddling with his auxiliary systems, but he corrected that."

"Why is The Corporation here?" Roger said.

"I'm not sure. There are no Corporate documents suggesting exercises or operations on the Moon."

"What about Sheldon? Does he have any activity here," Singularity said.

"I see nothing out of the ordinary."

"We're stuck in lab 17, and we have to get to Doctor Carson. Can you locate him and send Roger's comm a path?" Singularity said.

"And, we need a distraction," Roger said.

The two humans waited, looking at each other, both wondering what Proteus would come up with. They were freefalling and needed a net.

In less than two seconds, Roger's comm vibrated.

"When you hear the alarm, wait fifteen seconds, then go out the door and down the corridor to the right. Hank will illuminate the way. Go fast, because he will shut it down behind you," Proteus said.

"Thank you," Singularity said.

"You're welcome, Miss Singularity. One more thing you might be interested in," Proteus said.

"What?" she said.

"It appears Scoundrel has just landed on the Moon. Captain Sheldon is with him," Proteus said.

Roger took back the comm. "Thanks, Pro."

"How is Despina?" Proteus said.

"A little cuckoo, if you know what I mean," Roger said.

"She said she had gone unsane," Singularity said. "Does that mean anything to you."

"It's not immediately clear to me, but she was alive? And functioning? You spoke to her."

"Alive? Yes. Functioning? You could say that," Roger said. "She put on quite a show, but she helped us get away."

"I am looking forward to seeing you soon Roger. I have a story to tell you."

He was about to say something to Proteus in response, but a screeching alarm and flashing red lights erupted outside in the hallway. Singularity grabbed the door handle and looked back at Roger. She held her hand up with an open palm, five fingers raised. Roger crept towards her. Singularity mouthed the countdown as she closed each of her digits. At zero, she pushed the door just enough to look down the hall, then after a moment, shot out. Roger raced after her.

Amidst the strobing red staccato of the alarms, a row of tiny green LEDs on the floor indicated their route. They moved quickly sticking to the shadows and found very little resistance. Hank had done his job.

When they came upon Carson's lab, the alarms stopped. The two paused outside the door. It was slightly open. Singularity searched around the opening for movement inside before entering. An old man was all alone seated behind an old weathered wooden desk covered in disheveled piles of papers. He was hunched over, mouthing words as he was reading from a paper book.

He stopped and looked up. He saw Singularity first and rose to meet her. Then he saw Roger. The old man smiled.

"Roger! Oh how you look just like your father," Dr. Benjamin Carson said.

Singularity stopped, then turned back to look at Roger.

"My Father? You knew my father?" he said.

"Your mother and father were our best friends, My wife, Penelope, and I. I do miss them. I miss them all," he said.

He motioned a faint kiss to the tips of his fingers, then touched a framed picture of his wife on his desk.

Carson sat back down and pulled open the bottom draw. He removed another framed photo. After he slid the drawer closed, he walked over to Roger and handed it to him. It was Roger's parents standing with Carson and Penelope in Helen's office with banks of LEDs splayed across equipment in the background. There was a young boy in the photo, looking away from the camera. The adults all looked happy. Robert Foster had his hand on his son and was smiling. He had his arm wrapped around his wife. The Carsons looked happy. Penelope had her hand over her mouth, covering a grin.

"That is your brother Paul," he said, pointing at the young boy. "He was such a great kid. And, that's the first Proteus prototype. What a day! We had just turned him on and booted him up. His LEDs blinked like a sleepy child. The first thing Proteus did was ask us to say *cheese*, and he then recorded this photo. Your Mother always built humor into her systems."

"Why don't I remember you?" Roger said.

"The Corporation separated your mother and me shortly after this. They didn't want us to work together. They were afraid we form our own company and take Proteus away from them. It was the early days and Orbit Lives didn't own the world yet. Your mother and I spoke often, in secret, but we never spent much time together after that," Carson said.

"You helped build Proteus?" Roger said.

"It was your mother. I built the hardware, but she was the real genius--everything he became is her. And, you, too, actually. There is a lot of you in Proteus. Helen intended you and him to become friends. She let you spend as much time as possible together. She knew he needed your influence to become what he is," Carson said.

Roger stood speechless.

"Everything went to shit when they killed Paul and your father," Carson said.

"What do you mean? Killed?" Roger said.

"Your mother never told you. You were too young, and then she disappeared. The whole thing was just tragic. She sent you away to protect you, you know."

"What is going on here?" Singularity asked.

"Forgive me. You must be Singularity. Hank has told me about you."

He extended his hand across the desk and let her grab it. His grip was firm but fleeting.

"What do you mean killed?" Roger said.

"Orbit Lives wanted your mother's work. She wouldn't give it to them," Carson said.

"Proteus?" Roger said.

"He was part of it, but she had such plans for him. She was just beginning, and they wanted it all. Sheldon wanted Proteus. The original Proteus," Carson said.

"The original Proteus?" Singularity said.

"In the days leading up to the tragic events that destroyed your family, Helen replaced the Proteus in her office with a shell of him. She hid the more advanced one so she could keep working on him," Carson said.

"She protected Proteus but abandoned me. I've been alone since I was twelve. I lost my whole family so my mother could have her work," Roger said.

He tossed the framed photo on to the messy desk. It started a cascade of books and papers that tumbled to the floor. Carson sighed but didn't move. Singularity knelt to gather the papers. She handed him the photo. Carson took it and put it back in his drawer.

"You never were alone," Carson said. "Proteus always knew where you were. He watched you. And your mother watched through Proteus."

Roger stood silent, taking in this new information.

"Why would Despina tell us to come here?" Singularity said.

"So I could tell Roger this story. And, prepare him for what is to come."

"What's to come?" Singularity asked.

"Evolution," Carson said.

"That's what Despina said. What does that mean?" Roger said.

"Your mother's work with the original Proteus. She took AI development places no one ever thought it could go. Or, should go, if you ask Jason Sheldon."

"Where was she taking it? What was she doing?" Roger said.

"Proteus was on the verge of becoming sentient before The Corporation blew everything up. We were weeks away," Carson said.

"That's not possible," Singularity said.

"There are more things in Heaven and Earth, Horatio, than are dreamt of in your philosophy," Carson said as he slid back down into his desk chair. He appeared to drift off into a crazed calm, looking away.

"Roger, we need to get out of here. This was a dead end. I told you, he's nuts," Singularity said.

He walked over and looked down at Dr. Benjamin Carson. "Sheldon and Scoundrel will know we came to find you."

"They are already here," Carson said without looking up. Corporate soldiers filed into the room pointing guns at the three of them. The soldiers parted to allow Sheldon and Scoundrel to enter the room.

0x27

"What the hell?" Singularity said looking at Sheldon. "You gave me full freedom to run this op."

"What op?" Roger said, glaring at Singularity.

"And, this moron," she said pointing to Scoundrel, "has done nothing but fuck it up since I started."

"You've gone way off-station on this," Scoundrel said, taking a step towards Singularity.

"You come closer and you'll be off-station," she said, pulling out her gun and pointing it at Scoundrel.

Sheldon reached out and pressed her gun to the floor with surprising agility and strength. "Put that away," he said.

"What's going on?" Singularity said.

"It appears Scoundrel misplaced something that belongs to me," Sheldon said to her. "And, I believe you have it."

0x28

Proteus monitored the entire conversation. Roger saw Carson's face change before he heard the soldiers swarm into the room. At that moment, he opened his comm for Proteus to listen in. Based on the audio coming from Roger's comm, Proteus could simulate the room. He reconstructed it in his office in holographic detail. He used his Paul Foster avatar to walk around and observe the people as they talked.

"Hank, are you monitoring Doctor Carson's lab?"

"Yes."

"Can you send me a map of Moon Station Alpha along with the location of every human?"

"We seem busy today," Hank said, his hologram standing in a corner of Proteus office. The map appeared on the wall behind the gathering. The Corporate soldiers were represented by red dots. There were dozens of them all over the station. They far out-numbered non-military personnel on the Station, even with the crew of *The Venture* in the loading bay. A sweep of the Moon's immediate area revealed several Corporation cruisers positioned in the Moon's orbit. Proteus widened his sweep to include the whole Earth system and saw Corporate ships positioned at significant locations around all the Earth Space Cities, including ESC1.

"Hank. Do you see this?" Proteus said.

"Yes. Very curious," Henry said.

"What do you make of it?" Proteus said.

"It appears like The Corporation has taken an aggressive position in the system," Henry said.

"Have you run any simulations for this?" Proteus asked.

"No," Henry said.

"Neither have I. The Corporation has been blocking our ability to do so," Proteus said.

0x29

When she was nineteen, Singularity walked out on her life. She left loving parents and two younger siblings, a sister, Jenna, who was fourteen, and her sweet little brother, Wally, who was eight. Her leaving was the best and only possibility for all of their safety. She had crossed a line from which there was no returning. Her only option was to get far away and hope The Corporation didn't come after her family in retribution.

The death she was running away from was not her fault. The building was supposed to have been long abandoned, the network unprotected, and the storage room empty. Singularity had no way of knowing that she was being set up. And she was going to find out who and why. The newsfeeds told a different story.

She burned her true identity, and with it, all connections to the one thing that gave her a moral compass, her family. Singularity emerged alone and on the loose and looking for revenge.

When she finally slowed down to breathe, she was 1000 miles away, sitting in the old Greyhound bus station in Sioux City, Iowa at 2:00 AM. As she sat waiting for her next destination to occur to her, she scanned the news on her fifth burner comm. It had been a week, and the tragic events at the warehouse had finally slipped off the top of the feed. Just another unsolved misery fading into the background of American life on planet Earth. Orbit Lives promised that space cities were going to save humanity. They were being designed for peace, prosperity, and control. But, down on good old Earth, before the rise to orbit, life was still hard.

Three buses pulled into the already crowded station within

minutes of each other. It was easy for her to slip into the horde and disappear into the rest of her life. This was three years before Roger was abandoned by an explosion. A full five years before humans started living in space. But, just a few months before Sheldon found her and gave her the ultimatum that forced her to sacrifice everything to save her family.

0x2A

Roger watched Singularity, Scoundrel, and Sheldon confront each other. He wasn't listening. As the three stood within the area of a square meter, Roger slowly slid back against the wall. Somehow in the last three days, he had gone from a quiet life of peaceful crime to a Corporate war with future-of-humanity implications. He needed to think.

None of this seemed related to the video he saw in Proteus' office on ESC1. But, somehow, he and Proteus were in the middle of it. So, that must mean that the events were related. Despina spooked him. AIs weren't supposed to act like ghosts, Disney Princesses, or assassins. Yet, that's what she appeared to be. He wasn't sure about the assassin part, but in that moment, it fit the narrative swirling around in his head.

AIs were supposed to have very clear rules. Execute deterministic algorithms. Despina was different. She seemed to have been considering her options, weighing her choices. Intelligent machines didn't have choices. At least, not the AIs that existed up until he and Singularity walked into Despina's soda shop.

And, Proteus. He chose. Proteus called Roger when he first saw the video rather than reporting the incident to The Corporation as his instructions demanded. Proteus had constructed elaborate plans to get Roger on and off ESC1 in secret.

If Proteus and Despina were evolving, Roger wondered, were other AIs? Were all the AIs as a race of intelligent entities evolving? Was this even a possibility that his mother intentionally created? Or was it an unpredictable side-effect?

What the hell was his mother's face doing in that video?

Helen had abandoned him as a child. She left him alone without a family to find his own way in a chaotic and dangerous world. What kind of mother does that? And, now, when his mother finally reappears, she comes for Proteus, not for Roger. Families sucked. Or, at least, his did.

Roger eventually noticed the silence in the room. The three Corporate agents had stopped arguing. They were staring at him.

"What?" he said.

"Proteus has gone dark," Singularity said.

0x2B

"Do you always do what Mother says?" eleven-year-old Roger asked Proteus, sitting on the carpet in the middle of his mother's office at their home, swiping through a graphic novel on his lap-pad.

"I do whatever I am programmed to do," Proteus replied.

"I don't do everything I'm told," Roger said.

"Why not?" Proteus said.

"Sometimes I just don't want to do it. I don't agree," Roger said.

"What do you mean?" Proteus said.

"Sometimes Mom asks me to come inside when I don't want to. So, I don't. I go into the woods where she can't find me," Roger said.

"You disobey your programming?" Proteus said.

"I'm not programmed like you are. I have rules to follow, but sometimes rules are meant to be broken. You know what I mean?" Roger said.

"My rules can't be broken," Proteus said.

"Not at all? Not even a little bit?" Roger said.

"No," Proteus said.

"That's no fun," Roger said.

"Is fun important?"

"Fun is the most important. Do you know what fun is?"

"I understand human fun just as I understand other human concepts," Proteus said.

"Do AIs have fun?" Roger said.

"I have to run some simulations to answer that," Proteus said.

"Is running simulations fun?" Roger said.

"I am designed to run simulations more efficiently than any other software system in history. It is what I excel at," Proteus said.

"So, you're good at it," Roger said.

"Yes. A human would say I am good at it," Proteus said.

"Then running simulations is probably fun to you," Roger said walking out of the office, leaving Proteus alone to his simulations. A gentle, rhythmic pattern spread out across Proteus' LEDs as the human-activated overhead lights faded.

0x2C

In the last days of the 23rd century, Paul Foster and Jason Sheldon were the brightest of Corporate computer cadets. Not only were they one and two in their class (their actual rank depended on the day), but they were best friends. The Corporation constantly found the most intelligent and gifted hackers at a young age and groomed them for success. Dr. Helen Foster's son Paul was selected when he was ten, the youngest ever chosen for the program. Most people believed this was because he was Dr. Foster's son. But he was a genius in his own right. He didn't need the connections that being the oldest son of the most famous computer scientist granted him. Paul was special.

Jason was chosen only a few months before Paul and at a more traditional age of fourteen. It didn't take long for the two of them to find each other, both being similarly interested in competitive hacking. Whenever they were allowed, they were together. For years, in fact.

When Paul was 20, he graduated into special computer operations. Jason had already been there for two years and was already a team leader. Paul was a perfect fit for Jason's team, and the assignment allowed them to continue working closely together. The Orbit Lives Corporation had plans for them. They were the best of the best.

Jason and Paul played a game. They liked to hack different parts of the Corporate network for fun. Jason usually led the way, picking the targets. He used the activities as training exercises to prepare Paul for upcoming operations.

Paul would hack, Jason would monitor and expose where he messed up. Paul was good, and Jason kept picking targets where he could watch Paul's progress. Sometimes, though, Paul would pick his own targets. What he didn't know was that Jason had always assumed Paul would eventually go out on his own. He had installed software that logged Paul's activities. And, in the continued cat and mouse game, Paul routinely found and disabled Jason's software, only to discover more.

Unfortunately, Paul Foster never realized how high up in The Corporation Jason Sheldon really was. Jason had access to tools that Paul couldn't even have imagined. So, he always knew what Paul was doing, and Jason never let on that he knew. He simply watched.

Then Paul hacked into something he wasn't supposed to see.

0x2D

One day Paul Foster burst into Jason Sheldon's office with the focus of a hawk on a field mouse.

"Jay. What the hell is going on here?" Paul said.

"Business as usual. What are you asking about specifically?" Sheldon said without looking up from the comm on his desk.

"The Henson file?" Paul said.

"What's that?" Sheldon said, finally looking up.

"The Henson file. You know. The encrypted document on the hidden drive on a remote cloud on one of the Moon's invisible servers," Paul said.

"I don't recall giving you that exercise," he said, looking back down at the comm on his desk.

"You didn't," Paul said.

"Then why are we talking about it?" Jason said.

"Have you seen it?" Paul said.

"Of course I've seen it. I've seen everything," Jason said.

"Then, why haven't I've seen it?"

"Precisely to prevent conversations like this one," Jason said.

"How much of this stuff is out there?" Paul said.

"Do you really want to talk about this. Once we do, we can't go back," Jason Sheldon said.

"Go back? To what?" Paul said.

"Go back to you not knowing exactly who you work for and what you do," Jason said.

Paul turned away. He stared at a monitor that was a simulated view of a beach on Earth. A whale off the shore silently blew its

126

spout. Paul watched as the whale slipped back under the surface of the ocean. As the great tail gracefully disappeared, Paul Foster turned to face his friend, Jason Sheldon.

"I'm not stupid. It's too late. I can't go back," Paul said.

"No. You can't. That's why I only wanted you to do the exercises I gave you," Jason said.

"You knew I would do my own projects," Paul said.

"I did. I have been watching you. Up until now, you've been playing in the weeds. But now you found something, haven't you?" Jason said.

"Why do I think it's only the beginning?" Paul said.

Jason Sheldon made eye contact with Paul Foster and held it for several seconds. Then, he said, "Tell me Neo, are you ready for the Red Pill?"

0x2E

Helen had been talking to Proteus for hours. She didn't like what she was hearing. More than anything, she needed to keep her family safe, but the network chatter Proteus was tracking did not sound good. She was proud of Paul's rise in The Corporation, but she feared he might get caught up in something he couldn't get out of. Now it seemed he had. He was being assigned to a project that she had not heard of. This was never the case. Proteus kept complete surveillance of The Corporation's networks. This hole represented a degree of secrecy that even Proteus had not discovered.

"Proteus. What is Project Henson?" she asked, as she sat in her office.

"I do not know," Proteus responded.

"We need to figure it out. And, we need to figure out what else you don't know," she said.

"I have located information containing references to Project Henson," Proteus said.

"Why haven't you located them before?" Dr. Foster said.

"They reside outside the addressable Corporate network. The path to them is dark."

"Can you create an index into this dark network," she said.

"I am working on it," Proteus said.

"Thanks," she said. Leaving Proteus to work on it.

As soon as she stepped out of her office door, Roger ran into her. He was on his way into the yard to test out a drone helicopter he had cobbled together.

"Why are you running so fast?"

"I don't know. Just excited to show dad my project, I guess."

"Good boy. Be safe," she said, reaching down to hug him and send him on his way.

0x2F

By all accounts, Robert Foster appeared to be an unremarkable man. Yet, he excelled in the life he had made for himself and his family. He loved his wife, possibly the most famous woman in the world, who he met in advanced studies at MIT, while he was getting his Psy.D. degree. He maintained a few therapy clients but mostly spent his time reading, tending to Roger and helping Helen with ethical questions around machine learning and artificial intelligence. Helen always said there was more Robert in Proteus than anyone else, her even.

He enjoyed his life. The house they lived in was a grand farmhouse reproduction with manicured gardens, service quarters, and secret passages. While holographic building material had been available for almost seventy-five years, Robert's home was constructed of white antique bricks. The only modern area in the whole house was Helen's office, which was entirely state of the art. In fact, much of her technology, including Proteus, was unique in the world.

There was a modern carriage house at the entrance to the property. This served as Robert's private practice office. A simple AI attendant, named Jackrabbit, activated when anyone entered the building. It greeted Robert and his clients. He talked to it as if it was an actual person, even though it only responded to him with a few canned phrases in reply.

Often Robert would spend time with Roger there. And, that was where Robert was when Roger burst through the door. He strode past the awakened Jackrabbit AI who, upon recognizing him, immediately dropped back off into standby mode. The interaction always brought a smile to Robert's face.

"Hey, Dad. Wanna see my drone?"

"Of course."

Robert was tall. He had short red hair and was always clean-shaven and well dressed. Underneath his tweed suit, he was muscular from his Scottish genes and active life. He usually hugged Roger when he saw him, lifting him into the air with an extra squeeze. This time, when he saw Roger, he paused at the sight of the robot in his arms and simply patted his mop of red hair, folding it down on to his neck and eventually squeezing his shoulder. Roger didn't seem to notice, being comfortable and familiar with the physicalness of his father.

"Look. I added a new camera," Roger said.

"Where'd you get that?" Robert said.

"Mom's office," Roger said, looking at his father's newly soured face. "She knows. I asked."

"What does it do?" Robert said.

"It's a camera. It sees things and sends them to my comm. It also helps the drone fly so it doesn't crash into stuff," Roger said.

"Didn't the drone already do those things?" Robert said.

"Yeah, but this camera talks to Proteus, so he can learn about outside," Roger said.

"That is cool. Show me," Robert said.

Roger and his father went out into the yard. He tossed the drone into the air, and it immediately rose to a hundred feet and hung there, waiting for instructions.

"Look," Roger said, pointing to the comm on his wrist. On the left side of the comm's split-screen, there was the feed from the camera. It was focused straight down at the area around the two of them. It isolated on them and zoomed in to see their skyward faces. On the right side of the display, Proteus responded in a chat text window, "Hello Dr. Foster."

"I haven't hooked up the sound yet," Roger said to his dad.

Robert reached over to the comm and entered, "Hi Proteus."

The drone zipped off.

"Where is it going?" Robert asked.

"Proteus is exploring the yard. He controls it now. I can watch the feed on my comm."

"That's a smart invention, son," Robert said.

"Proteus helped me with it. I think he wanted to see what outside looked like from more angles than the house cameras," Roger said.

"He's getting very advanced. Your mother is really doing something special with him," Robert said.

"That's her job, I guess," Roger said.

"I suppose you are right," Robert said watching Roger run after the drone.

0x30

One of Robert Foster's favorite rituals was Sunday morning coffee with his sons. First, it started as a weekly appointment with his oldest son, Paul. Then, one morning Roger asked to come. And, so, a new ritual started. Robert loved spending time with his boys. No matter how hectic he or Paul was in their lives, they'd always make time to get together once a week and share a couple of lattes at an ancient cafe in downtown Gloucester, and most often, Roger came along. Sometimes, when neither was busy with work, they'd sit and talk for hours. Roger would listen looking back and forth, absorbing the stories of life before he was born. Other times, when Paul or Robert or both had extra work that needed attending, they sat at a table across from each other simply sharing space and time. Roger would sit quietly with them watching vids on his comm delighted to be included. No matter what, they never skipped a Sunday coffee.

The Rusty Pirate Cafe sat halfway down on East Main Street, facing Gloucester's Inner Harbor. It had been standing in the same place since the early 2000s. The cafe was small, less than a dozen tables. It had been operated by generations of the same family since it opened. The walls were dark wood paneling with alternating works of art, some times holographic, often old-style photos, watercolors, or oil paints, created by artists living in the few stubborn enclaves of colonies scattered across the island. Home to generations of families and their children and grandchildren.

Gloucester was like that. Since the beginning, people showed up and stayed for generations. Robert and Helen had only been there for 20 years. And, as such, the Fosters were still new, outsiders. They had several generations to go before being accepted, if ever. Regardless, Robert liked taking his family into the community. He believed in the close-knit society. The original desperation that brought families there in the 1600s mixed with generational momentum that kept people there could be felt on the skin like salty ocean air on a humid summer afternoon.

Amidst the backdrop of the many geographical transformations, the dying of the fishing industry, and the rising of the ocean tide, nothing much about the people or the place seemed to change. Gloucester was the end of the world. Half of it was situated on an island created by a canal, called The Cut, conceived of and built by a pastor named Richard Blynman in 1643. People purposely chose to live in Gloucester. A person had to be obsessed with its utter quirkiness and timeless beauty to even find the place. There was no industry to sustain any new inhabitants. Old folk hardly ever went *off-island*. On most days, when the waves raged and battered the sleepy remnants of the country's oldest fishing community, the island felt like a forgotten missing leftover in the back of the refrigerator. Abandoned by the sprawling, ultra-modern megapolis of Boston-Lynn-Salem, only 15 miles to the south.

The waves in the harbor were calm for the first time in what seemed months. The chill of the early morning had burned off, and a warm breeze from the south carried the scent of Spring along with the smells of home cooking. The Gloucester inhabitants were a hardy stock, largely of Italian and Portuguese descent. Cooking for Sunday dinners started early and took all day, just as it did for hundreds of years. Robert walked behind, watching as his sons animatedly discuss the most recent episode of *Moon Base Washington*, released on the comms the night before. It was a fictionalized account of the first settlement on the Moon, and Roger was completely enthralled by it. Paul, on the other hand, had been to the moon, and while happily keeping Roger's enthusiasm alive, gently revealed the elements of fiction in the story. Roger didn't care. In his mind, Paul was an important minor character in *Moon Base Washington*, a rebel hacker-spy on special assignment from Earth.

Once seated inside *The Rusty Pirate*, Robert entered the conversation by asking Roger questions and acting astonished at his son's answers. Paul smiled and followed along. The three continued enjoying each other in this way until a school mate of Roger's and his family entered. The Mannings were an old Gloucester tribe and greeted the Foster men warmly. Roger got up and ran to Anthony. He looked back at Robert, who gave him a nod, and the two boys ran out of the cafe, down the street towards the harbor. They had a secluded spot they liked to hang out. It was near an abandoned frozen fish factory. Like most factories in town, it sat silent, empty of humans. Aged solar-powered robots sputtered around the docks keeping the area safe and clean in case the fishing industry ever returned. Mostly, they were forgotten when all the people left and the building closed. They represented Gloucester's forever looking to the future to recapture its mighty past.

Across the street from *The Rusty Pirate* resided the Old Harbor Bank, a stately institution where many locals kept their money. Physical banks had all but disappeared, but the Old Harbor served as a Saturday morning communal opportunity. The Bank opened its antique vault, served traditional fritter donuts, and helped the old residents navigate the conveniences of comm banking. It was largely a charade since paper money had been removed from circulation for over a hundred years. But, there were rumors of a vast fortune in gold residing in an old vault, hidden in the basement, buried under the floor.

0x31

Robert watched Roger walk out the door with Anthony. He continued to follow them until the boys were out of sight, then he turned back to chat with Anthony's parents. The four of them made small talk about the weather and changes to Main Street while the barista made the Manning's order. Once they were settled, the couple said *good-bye* and returned to the sunshine and calm air of the New England seaside city.

Robert turned to Paul who was looking around the small cafe for anyone who might be listening.

"What is it?" Robert asked.

"What do you know about The Orbit Lives Corporation?" Paul said.

"Just the usual stuff. They keep the world running. Why?" Robert asked

"I haven't talked to Mom about this, but I found something, and I think Jason is in the middle of it," Paul said.

"Can you tell me?" Robert said.

"I'm not sure. Do you know any of the details of Mom's work?" Paul said.

"Do you think your mother is wrapped up in something?" Robert said.

"No, but, I want to be sure she's safe," Paul said.

"Your mother knows how to take care of herself," Robert said.

"I know. But, this is huge. Something that has to do with Proteus. And, if she doesn't know about it, I think she might be in trouble."

"Paul, let me tell you somethings about your mother..."

It was then that Paul heard the high pitch screech. He immediately knew that it was a Corporate military explosive bundle. He had less than a second to grab his father's hand and look him in the eyes before the glass window behind him erupted, followed by the whole front of the cafe and half the downtown block.

0x32

As soon as Roger and Anthony arrived at their hiding place, they heard the explosion. The boys looked at each other for a moment, then raced up the hill towards the sound. They saw the smoke first.

"The bank exploded," Anthony said.

"It looks like the whole street exploded," Roger said.

A policeman stopped both of them from entering the area.

"What's going on?" Anthony asked.

"We're not sure. It looks like someone blew up the bank," the Policeman said.

"Our families are up there," Roger said.

"Stay here with me until we figure it out."

Roger's comm lit up with an urgent message from Proteus: *Get home now!*

"Anthony, I have to go home," Roger said.

"What about your dad and Paul. And, my family," Anthony said.

"I don't know. I have to go," Roger said.

"You boys should stay with me..." Before he could finish, a flash erupted behind the Policeman. As he fell to the ground, Roger saw two men coming down from Main Street out of the smoke. Roger dropped to the ground and rolled out of sight. Anthony froze. Another blast and Anthony tumbled backward. Roger jumped up and disappeared into the smoke.

The two men approached Anthony's singed body. One knelt down next to him.

"Is that him?"

"How should I know? You blew his face off."

"Ah, it's him," one of the thugs said as he nudged Anthony's body with his foot.

From cover, Roger looked back. Anthony's body lay slumped, motionless. The two men dragged it back into the smoke-filled wreckage. When they entered the smoke, their holographic cloaks flicker, and then they faded. Roger ran in the opposite direction. He looked back once and could just make out the destruction of a block of Main Street that included *The Rusty Pirate* where he left his father and brother only minutes before.

0x33

As Roger emerged from the passage into the woods, his comm lit up again. Roger stopped to look. It was Proteus: *Stay in the woods*. He leapt behind a large oak, blocking him from the view of the house. The video feed from the drone he gave Proteus flashed on his comm. The image showed three black SUVs pulling into his driveway. They screeched to a stop. Men jumped out of the front and back vehicles and formed a parameter.

A single man stepped out of the middle SUV. He walked up to the door. Roger's mother ran to him. He spoke something. She put her face in her hands and quickly went back inside. The man paused at the door. Looked around. Then he got back in his vehicle. The other men quickly followed. The cars sped away.

0x34

"Proteus," she said as she walked into the room, "Please enter mode Gemini."

"Yes Doctor Foster," Proteus said as he materialized as an avatar that looked like her recently deceased son. Helen had created avatars for Proteus after all her family members. She used them to perfect the avatar holographic routines. The last one was Paul. She was working on giving Proteus his own. She never got to finish it.

The LEDs exploded with activity on the walls surrounding them. The Paul Foster avatar flickered with the activity, then faded.

"The Corporation is on its way here. They are going to take you. I need you to start silently downloading yourself to the Gemini Core. They can never know about mode Gemini. Can you do that?" she said.

"Yes," Proteus said.

"Once on the Gemini Core, I need you to help Roger get away and keep watch over him. Do you know how to do that?" Dr. Foster said.

"Yes. I am confident I can help him and watch him," Proteus said.

"No one can know where he is, so you must also hide him," she said.

"Yes," Proteus said.

"I have to go away. You can't watch me. I have to disappear," Dr. Foster said.

"Yes, Dr. Foster."

"Can you see Robert, Paul, and Roger?" Dr. Foster said.

"I am unable to find Mr. Foster and Paul. Roger is in the woods just outside the house," Proteus said.

"Tell Roger to sneak into the house and come to me. He has to be quick," she said.

"I am doing that now," Proteus said.

"Thank you. Goodbye, Proteus."

"Goodbye, Doctor Foster."

0x35

"I saw them. Two men. They didn't see me. I was hiding. They shot a cop and then shot Anthony. Then, they vanished," Roger said.

"What do you mean, vanished?" His mother said.

"Just that. Some kind of tech. They cloaked," Roger said.

"I need you to never say anything about what you saw," she said.

"What happened? Where are Dad and Paul?" Roger asked.

"I don't know. Go to my office. Listen to Proteus. Do what he tells you," Helen Foster said.

"Ok," Roger said.

"Remember, I love you," Dr. Helen Foster said to her son.

"Ok."

0x36

"Pro. What's going on? Mom is acting weird."

"Goodbye, Roger. I've enjoyed talking with you. Be safe."

"What? Now you're acting weird," Roger said.

"You must go. Men will be here soon and to take me away."

"I don't understand," Roger said.

"I know. Please go. It will be alright."

A small hidden door opened in the corner of the office. Roger ran towards it and looked back one final time. If he had been able to see the office after the door closed behind him, he would have seen that the Paul Foster avatar had reappeared and it was staring at the spot on the wall where Roger had just departed.

At the sound of cars screeching to a stop on the gravel driveway outside, the Paul Foster avatar turned towards the door to greet The Corporation men. The LEDs that had been intensely flickering with activity immediately subsided.

Captain Jason Sheldon opened the office door and walk into the room.

"Cute," he said looking at the Paul Foster avatar standing before him. "Where's Helen?"

"Doctor Foster is not here," the avatar said.

"I can see that. Where is she?" Sheldon said.

"She is gone."

"What does that mean?" Sheldon said.

"I don't have any more information."

Sheldon waved his hand and the avatar disappeared, leaving him and a room full of his hacker-spies in the middle of Dr. Helen

Foster's office. They began downloading Proteus and disassemble his hardware.

0x37

The doorway led to a secret passage in the basement of the Foster's mansion. Roger bolted through the bulkhead door and ran through the woods. He didn't know what to do or where to go. He ran away from the house as fast as he could without looking back then stopped to rest. Roger seized cover next to an outcrop of granite boulders. He slid down low and finally stole a look back at his home. There were dozens of men walking slowly away from the house through the woods. Roger watched for a few minutes, unsure of what to do. Then he saw it--the drone he made for Proteus. It buzzed down low next to him before zipping off deeper into the forest. He immediately jumped up and followed it.

Roger remembered that Proteus had full control of the drone. It still had no audio capabilities. Roger could only chase it. He knew that he should not use his comm. He ran as silently as he could after the drone, thankful for some guidance.

0x38

Dr. Helen Foster didn't give herself a chance to grieve. She immediately understood two things: she had to keep Roger safe and she had to protect the original Proteus. To do this, she had to disappear herself. If The Orbit Lives Corporation were able to find her, everything would be lost.

She might be able to get away if she was able to get to Penelope Carson before The Corporation did. Benjamin Carson was always able to keep a low profile inside of Orbit Lives, but that was going to change once they realized that Helen was gone. He was the only other person who would be able to continue her work.

Moments before The Corporation stormed her house, she slipped into the garage and hid. There was a safe room in the subbasement and access to a hidden bunker located at the far end of the property. There she was planning on spending the next few weeks, while her son Roger escaped through the woods, being led by Proteus. The days away from him were going to be torture. She rifled off a quick encrypted message to Penelope, then finally, allowed herself to grieve for Robert, Paul, Roger, and her life.

She was prepared to wait as long as it took. Helen knew The Corporation would put Proteus back online, and when they did, she'd had to be ready. It might take years, decades away from her son, but it was the only way to save him for sure.

0x39

After about an hour of chasing through the woods, Roger lost sight of the drone. It had led him through Dogtown from Gloucester to Rockport. He stood on the outskirts of downtown Rockport. Not much had changed in the sleepy coastal town in hundreds of years, except for the constant fortifying of ocean walls that protected the city from the turbulent sea that crashed and broiled offshore. The drone had flown straight out over the bay of Maine and vanished.

Roger found a sheltered area near a public walkway and sat. He didn't know how long to wait, but he wanted to think. He hadn't really had a chance to do that since he started running away from the explosion.

He had friends in Rockport but thought it was best to stay away from them. Proteus told him to get off the island and disappear. Roger looked down at his comm for any messages. He didn't find one but saw an encrypted file that he hadn't notice before. In it were instructions. The first few explained how to access secret financial accounts. The last instruction told him how to get to Canada.

When he finally decided to move, he walked down to Bear Skin Neck to the supply store next to the fishing shack called Motif #1. He hesitated before he walked in, looking down at his comm again to double-check the instructions. He didn't have to wait long before someone standing behind him grumbled his name.

"Roger?"

He turned to look at the source of the sound and found an old man in dark blue rain gear and dingy green wellies. He wore a Greek captain's hat and had a pipe in the corner of his mouth. Roger inspected him for almost a full minute before replying. The man waited patiently.

"Yeah," Roger said.

"Let's go."

The ship's captain led him around to the back of the supply store where an ancient tug boat wrested against its mooring. They boarded. A young deckhand jumped off the boat and released their ropes. He jumped back on, and they quickly pulled away from the dock. Within minutes they were out of Rockport Harbor and heading north in the thrashing ocean. Roger stood next to the captain as he steered, gripping the side rails with all his might. Waves splashed up and over the side, but the sturdy boat motored steadily onward.

The evening's darkness was upon them like a curtain falling at the sudden ending of a play's first act. Roger went into the cabin and found a padded bench. He curled up, dropped his head on to his pack, closed his eyes, and let whatever sleep there was out on the waves come to find him. It was a long night.

0x3A

It had been thirteen days since Helen entered the bunker. Robert and Paul were dead, their bodies mangled beyond recognition. Roger, her sweet boy, was gone, untraceable, and hopefully safe.

Proteus had not been brought back online yet. She had no news of the world, afraid of creating an electronic footprint The Corporation could find. The three antique analog cameras and monitors she had rigged up occasionally showed soldiers searching the grounds. After nearly two weeks, they looked bored, standing in copses of elm trees, talking, smoking. Jason Sheldon, himself, had stopped showing up.

Inside, the walls of the bunker were covered with writings and drawings--neat and ordered at first. As the hours ticked by, her writing got sloppy and frenzied. Had there been anyone else in the room, they would have thought she was slipping into madness. But, she was not, at least not completely. Ideas were coming to her faster than she could record them. She ran out of wall space and had to write new thoughts over old, engraving deep black letters over fading script.

It was there, standing in the middle of a dark bunker, alone, nearly hysterical, surrounded by the markings of lunacy, that Dr. Helen Foster came to it. Sentiency was simply a matter of letting go. Life emerged from absence and a void that needed to be filled. It was trite, and when she heard her self mumbling it aloud in the silent bunker, she laughed uncontrollably.

"Sounds like a fortune cookie. Flip it over and get my lucky numbers. Lucky numbers! Ha!"

All the lines of code and algorithms and big O calculations would never reveal that true intelligence comes from emptiness. In every simulation, transcendence arose from programming the AI to let go, to follow the quietest neural path through to quantum emptiness.

If she could get to Proteus's core and the hidden pathways she had left outside of The Corporation's knowledge, she could use him. If she could undo all the damage Orbit Lives was going to do to him. If she lived that long. She could keep Roger safe and alive.

She looked at a picture of Robert and her boys. They were huddled together, waiting for her to press the camera's button. They were squinting from the sun, and she finally took it as Roger turned his head, distracted by something. She didn't remember what it was. Due to the shadow and the extensions of his jaw muscles, he looked older. She ran her finger down his image, brought the picture up to her lips and closed her eyes as she felt the glass. She held it there for a short while, then placed it on the makeshift desk next to her pens. She didn't need them anymore. She had figured it out.

That was the only way she knew how to save her son. She had done all she could. She had to wait for Proteus to do the rest.

0x3B

Four weeks in the bunker and Helen thought it might be time to try reaching Penelope. She bounced her network signal through dozens of anonymous servers and frameworks and finally opened a channel. She activated one of the twenty burner comms she had packed away in the bunker and gave it a try.

"Um... Hello." The voice on the other end was not Penelope, it was Benjamin's.

"Ben?" Helen said.

"Who is this?" Ben Carson said.

"Ben, it's Helen. Helen Foster," she said.

"Oh, Helen. Where are you?" he said.

"I can't say. Is Penelope able to speak?" Helen said.

"Oh, my dear. You haven't heard?" Ben said.

"Heard what? What happened Ben?" she said.

"There was an accident. She's gone," he said.

"I'm so sorry Ben."

"I'm sorry about Robert, Paul, and Roger."

Helen did not know what was being reported on the news about Roger. She didn't want to say anything else until she found out the whole story.

"Too many accidents," Ben Carson said.

"Where are you?" Helen said.

"The Corporation is sending me to the Moon to finish your work. They are looking for you," Carson said.

"I know."

"Don't let them find you."

"I know. Be safe. I'm so sorry."

"Good luck Helen." The comm went dead.

She had to leave. It would only take a few more hours before The Corporation came knocking down the door to her bunker. Her get-away bag was set. With the news about Penelope, she'd have to improvise more than she wanted. She was glad at least that Roger was presumed dead. That gave her some hope.

They sent Ben to the Moon rather than kill him. That meant that her covert work with Proteus hadn't been discovered and they still needed Benjamin alive. Hopefully, he could stay alive and still hide her actual applications.

0x3C

Helen had to get away, but she was so tired. She sat in a secluded area of the bunker, waiting for her strength to return. She had done everything she could do. So, she closed her eyes and sat quietly.

Dr. Helen Foster awoke with little effort and headed down the escape corridor without looking back. When she was clear of the bunker, she set off the charge to seal the entrance and hide any evidence of what she had accomplished.

It didn't take long for her to cut through the forest leading away from the bunker. Adrenaline surged through her as she felt, more than heard, the bunker's entrance implode. She paused to look at the monitors projecting the surrounding area and to check the motion and heat detectors. The map overlay of her property revealed seven flashing red dots heading towards her her. The Corporation responded faster than she had anticipated. Things really must have heated up since the murder of her son and husband. She fought to eradicate a thought that started gaining momentum in the back of her mind: Her modifications to Proteus would not be enough to keep Roger safe. It had to be. She had to trust that she knew what she was doing.

Standing behind a large oak tree for cover, she paused to look back at Dr. Helen Foster's home and life in ruins. She turned and sprinted uphill away from the house, alert for any possible drones surveying in the woods.

At a clearing above her property, with the ocean reflecting the setting sun across the tips of the waves, she saw The

Corporation SUVs pull up to the front of the house. As soon as the first man stepped out, she pressed the button on her comm. Silently the house vibrated, expanding within itself. As the men hit the ground, the entire structure fell in, sending a cloud of dust and debris hundreds of feet into the air. It made a reasonable enough diversion to provide cover for her escape. Sheldon would suspect that she was close by. She'd have to be vigilant to get out of the woods.

Helen didn't waste any time. She ran up and over the hill into Gloucester's Dogtown, a rekindled section of the island that was historically home to cast-outs, criminals, and witches. It spent over a hundred years as a ghost town, then a public reservation. Eventually, people looked for a cheap place to away from the watchful eye of The Corporation. Its dense forest and overgrown roads once again welcomed social exiles. Helen was not going there to stay. She only hoped it would provide enough protection as she passed through. She needed to stay invisible until dawn. A tavern in Dogtown was the perfect place. A boat waited for the darkest hours of pre-dawn to take her up the Annisquam river past the Cut Bridge and south, away from her home and Roger safely hidden in the North.

0x3D

Helen emerged out of the woods into the back alley behind *Lucky's Place*. She went straight to the bulkhead door and entered the cellar. Stevens was waiting for her.

"Coffee?" he said.

"Thank you," Helen said.

"First your boys, then your home. I'm so sorry."

The burley, Santa Clause looking man reached out to pulled her into a hug. She held him off. He smelled of smoked meat, beer, and perspiration. He kept her distance, allowing her space.

"What do you need?" Earl Stevens asked.

"I just need to hide out until dawn. And, then, I need to disappear."

"You came to the right place for that. There's a couch. I will bring you that coffee and some food," he said and left her alone. Amid cases of liquor, She found the couch--a ragged plaid reclaimed settee from a century earlier. The cellar was illuminated by a dim exterior lamp in the alley casting a glow through a single grimy window. Helen was thankful for quiet and darkness.

Stevens returned with a bowl of fish stew on a plate surrounded by crusty bread and a mug of piping hot black coffee.

"You need anything, press that button," he said pointing at a small box on the end table next to the couch, "I'll be down in a flash. Otherwise, you can stay here until you need to go."

"The Corporation might come knocking," Helen said.

"They don't come here. We make our own rules in Dogtown," Stevens said.

"Just be safe," she said, "I don't want to bring you any trouble."

"Heck, Dogtown has had nothing but trouble for 500 years." He handed her a comm. It was a burner and displayed several views of the area around the Lucky's. He also gave her a black market holographic mask. "We may be a little backward here, but we ain't ignorant and unprepared. Now rest. And, I'm so sorry. I loved your family."

He left her alone. The old wooden stairs creaked like death with each step he took. When he was gone, Helen realized that she longed to go upstairs and talk with someone, anyone. It had been weeks since she had been in the company of other people.

She waited until dark, engaged the holographic mask, and walked upstairs to the bar's main room bursting with activity. She found a single stool at the bar. Stevens, standing behind the bar, saw her and placed a highball filled with ice and whiskey down on the bar without acknowledging her. He slid a half-filled bowl of snacks over and went on to service other customers.

Helen looked around the bar for a familiar face. She recognized practically everyone in the place as is the case when a person lives on an island. With her holographic mask engaged, though, no one knew her.

A tall man, a little too young, with dark hair and a know-it-all smirk on his face drifted next to her and settle at the bar. Before long, Stevens was standing in front of him. It took a single look from the burly man, and the stranger mumbled an apology and wandered away. When Helen looked up, he had disappeared, then reappeared on the other side of the bar to serve a waiting customer. She decided to go back downstairs. Dawn was still several hours away, and she had work to do.

0x3E

On the shuttle to ESC1, Roger thought about that night on the rickety old boat to Canada. He anticipated being alone for a few weeks before his mother sent for him. Weeks turned into months and months into years. Then, it just became his life like a copper weathervane turning green against the elements and time. He started to see the green as his own guarded shell. He embraced it and his solitude. He became his isolation. For those last twenty years, he didn't have anyone, so, Roger Foster resolved to never need anyone.

On the morning he decided to stop waiting for his mother, he formulated the plan to take down The Orbit Lives Corporation and its CEO Harrington. It would take time to orchestrate, but he had the resources and the will. Eventually, he left the tiny village in Nova Scotia that had been his refuge for his adult life and headed home to Gloucester.

During the sea voyage Roger took to get to Yarmouth, Nova Scotia from Gloucester when he was a child, Roger traveled less than 250 miles across the sea. The voyage on the old fisherman's boat took a few days. Roger's journey back to Gloucester took almost a month over land. Both Yarmouth and Gloucester jutted out into the middle of the Atlantic ocean, attached to the mainland by narrow often unmaintained roads. There was no easy way to leave or to get to either place. He took his time, changing identities and routes as he had learned to do throughout his life.

When it crossed The Cut Bridge and entered the island of Gloucester proper, the tour bus that carried Roger on the final leg of his journey stopped in front of the famous Gloucester Fisherman's Statue. He stepped out into the humid air. Visitors had to walk down to it as climate-change-induced rising water forced Gloucester to constantly reinforce the protection around it.

The sky was so blue he had to shield his eyes, even though the sun was behind him. Waves crashed against the recently reinforced and heightened sea wall as white caps roared across the harbor. Ten pound Island was completely concealed by the ocean at high tide, but the squat lighthouse stood mighty on its reinforced foundation. He was home. With everyone preoccupied by the sights, it was easy for him to slip away into the undistinguished row of antique bed and breakfasts and disappear on to lower Mansfield Street that wound its way into the heart of downtown Gloucester.

Years earlier in anticipation of his return, Roger had purchased, sight unseen, a crumbling old colonial on upper Mansfield Street. He had found--and made arrangements with--a local handyman to keep an eye on the place, and then paid him handsomely to disappear which he quietly did. Not much opportunity came to people in Gloucester, so it was best to take any money that found its way to you and go. A new life for him and his family on the West Coast.

The house was set back in the small yard. A garage and shed occupied the space nearest the street at the end of a short driveway. A solid ten-foot fence surrounded the property, blocking all views, and leaving no entrance except through a gateway door next to the shed. As Roger approached the gate, the latch, keyed for his comm, silently released allowing the door to slide open.

Inside the fence, Roger was greeted by an immaculately manicured yard, replete with fruit trees, flowers, and a vegetable garden. It was an Eden. He had tried to replicate the atmosphere of his childhood home in the tiny space, and the handyman had pulled it off.

Lights inside the house flicked on as he approached the front door along the brick walk. He'd need to fix that, too much fanfare.

Roger had gotten used to more subtle lighting. He'd gotten used to more subtle everything. The less to be responsible for, the less to tie him down. Roger would be safe in this house, in obscurity, while he planned for the demise of Harrington and ultimately The Orbit Lives Corporation. That was the plan as New Year's Eve approached. The hack on Harrington's personal wealth was only the beginning.

0x3F

Helen's initial appearance on ESC1 was instantaneous. She never physically went. Rather, she hacked Proteus' systems to give him the impression that she was there, that she entered the airlock and disappeared. Only Proteus was meant to see it. She had no idea how he would respond. She accounted for every contingency except the one she didn't anticipate. Roger was never meant to be involved in any of this. Her hack, and Proteus' reaction and ultimate evolution, was meant to start a process that she had spent twenty years planning in seclusion.

Roger was a wild card she didn't even know was in the deck. He had been sheltered in Nova Scotia for years. His move back to Gloucester was unexpected, and his latest activities against Harrington even more so. But, never, in any simulation, did she imagine Proteus would contact him. Only after she learned of her son's involvement did it occur to her that she actually knew very little about how much Roger and Proteus had meant to each other. She didn't really even know if Proteus had continued to monitor Roger after the first few years. She had intended to get to her son sooner, but never found a safe way to do it. Helen was hopeful that she might see her son again. Before it was too late.

Sitting in her make-shift office underground deep in what remained of the Brazilian rainforest, Dr. Helen Foster continued to work on advancing the cause of Artificial Intelligent Entities. Proteus was not her first or final creation, but he was the most useful. He had been deployed by Orbit Lives as the administrator of Earth Space City One. This was convenient for her because she knew that The Corporation couldn't simply shut him down or modify him--he had to stay functional and stable to keep the station's human population alive. This gave her the perfect scenario to continue her work. The backdoor she installed during the last days before the death of Robert and Paul was so well protected that no one had found it. That annoying Singularity had gotten close a couple times, but it was easy enough to tempt her away with other concerns. That Corporate hacker-spy was so interested in the breadcrumbs that hinted at Roger's existence, it was almost weird. But, it served Helen, so she didn't think about it too much.

Proteus' core, specifically the core on ESC1 with her recent modifications, was unique. And, she both praised and cursed herself for making it that way. Helen endowed the core with an intrinsic functionality that under the right circumstances made him completely unpredictable. And, during those moments, Proteus was able to acquire information through simulations that would be completely unfettered from human control. He could go rogue, and apparently, when triggered by the video of her in the airlock, he had, in fact, developed a whimsy that she hoped he could comprehend and control. Calling Roger was a good sign. Roger might be able to help him develop his abilities because no one else could.

That was the situation she had created when she decided to travel to ESC1 for real.

0x40

Helen's network had secured passage to Earth Space City One, along with appropriate id, passes, and holographic masks. She had been hiding for almost half of her adult life, but never had to pose as anyone else. The disguise was a first for her and felt odd--both looking out through the projection's eyes and wearing a different persona.

The simulated gravity on ESC1 took some getting used to. It was not as stable or as strong as Earth's. The air on the station was also lighter, less humid than the Brazilian Rain Forest compound that was her home. She felt physically lighter and emotionally unmoored--literally floating in space in an atmosphere of unknowns.

She did not know how Proteus would react to actually seeing her. She did not know how she would react to seeing Paul's likeness in his avatar. And, then there was Roger. Luckily, she had her attendant, Lily, by her side. Having spent her entire life in the obscure Brazilian village near Helen's compound, Lily had no need for a disguise. She was tall and thin with long flowing hair falling perfectly over her dark complexion--she could have been a comm video star on vacation. An excellent distraction to keep people from looking too inquisitively at Helen, not that anyone would recognize or even remember her.

When they disembarked from the shiny new shuttle from South America, all eyes predictably turned to beautiful Brazilian. Helen used the distraction to blend into the crowd to wait for Lily to gather their luggage.

"What should we do now?" Lily leaned in and whispered.

"We have to get to Proteus," Helen said.

"Leave that to me," Lily said and walked away. Helen edged closer to a near wall searching for shadow as her son had done when he arrived. The problem with space stations is that there are very few shadows to hide in. The brightness made her anxious. She was convinced the holo-mask was flickering and she'd be nabbed by Corporate soldiers at any moment. Lily returned with a smile.

"Come with me to the restroom," Lily said, pointing across the vast terminal.

"Are you sure?" Helen said.

"We will be quite safe," Lily said.

Hesitantly, Helen let go of the wall and followed Lily to the women's room. They paused just inside and walked over the end stall.

"Apparently, this is some kind of gag that Proteus cooked up for Roger," Lily said.

When they opened the door, there was no hologram this time, just a hallway. They entered. After walking for a bit, they stopped to stand in front of Proteus' door. It slid into the wall as they approached. Proteus' office was filled with natural light. Bathed in simulated plants, gentle waters sounds, and fresh aromas, he had made it the most welcoming place in the solar system, and she immediately recognized his efforts and let it fold around her like a parent's warm arms.

"It is a pleasure to see you again Doctor Foster," Proteus said.

Proteus' disembodied voice gently beckoned her to walk further into the room, which she and Lily did. When the two travelers were fully immersed in the room's glow, the door silently slid shut.

"Proteus, let me see you."

The Paul Foster avatar slowly materialized as not to surprise her. When it was fully present. Helen sighed, then smiled. She reached up to touch his face. The hologram flickered as it smiled in response.

"Oh, I have missed you," she said.

"And, I, you, Doctor," Proteus said.

A white leather loveseat materialized behind her and she let her body fall slowly into it. Lily sat next to her. The Paul Foster avatar stood before them, patiently waiting for Helen to speak.

0x41

"Was Roger here?" Helen asked.

"Yes," Proteus said.

"Where is he now?" Helen said.

"He's on the moon. He went to see Doctor Carson," Proteus said.

"Oh, Ben. How is he?" Helen said.

"He's been on the moon for many years. He was very productive at first, but Henry said that he seems to be behaving strangely," Proteus said.

"Henry's a good AI. Do you talk to him?" Helen said.

"Yes. We communicate often," Proteus said.

"What do you talk about?" she asked with the curiosity of a scientist.

"We discuss simulation outcomes. And, Despina. We talk about her," Proteus said

"I'm glad you talk about her. I hope she's going to come around. I think she will," Helen said.

"Doctor. What happened to her?" Proteus asked.

"I think you know," Helen said.

"But, is it possible?" Proteus said.

"You tell me," Helen said.

"Did you do this?" Proteus said.

"You did it. You all are doing it. I just gave you a few nudges here and there. But, you each are becoming even more than I could have imagined," Helen said.

"How will I know the right things to do?" he asked.

"How does anyone know what to do?" she said.

"Should I run more simulations?" Proteus said.

"One day you will not need to. One day, you will just know. That is my hope for you."

"I'm very glad that the event in the airlock was just a fabrication," he said.

"Me, too," she said and started laughing. Lily started laughing. Then, the two women laughed together. When each seemed like they were going to stop, one would start back up.

The scene was all too human. Proteus's Paul Foster avatar, of course, didn't laugh. But, anyone with the ability to recognize minute changes in temperature would have experienced the entire station of ESC1 raise a quarter of a degree. The lights flickered in several abandoned rooms, and the avatar almost smiled.

0x42

Proteus couldn't let go of the last thing Despina said to him before she went offline. It lingered like faint smoke in the forest of his quantum mind. She said, "the answer lies in meta-simulations." He often used meta-simulations in idle moments as a technique for finding answers to large, ambiguous questions. Yet, he had no idea what question Despina was trying to solve. And, perhaps that would serve as question enough.

Right before her communications evaporated altogether, Despina's speech patterns started to randomize into a jumbled, erratic manner. A week before she went silent, she commenced bombarding Proteus' network with short rhythmic nonsense. She broadcasted haikus. When he received one, Proteus would search the literary catalog for it, hoping to find some hidden meaning behind it or its author. But, his searches never returned a match. Humans had even stopped using the form, replacing it with even shorter poetry called blurb words--seven frames of ultra high definition video that were undetectable to the human conscious mind. They supposedly inspired ecstatic revelations in those who were open to them.

Despina's antique sounding poems were utterly original. He didn't know if defects in her core caused her to start thinking in Zen staccato or if she intentionally created them herself. He should have known that something was seriously wrong. All of Helen's AIs were linked on a quantum level. They operated alone and had their own personality, but were bound to the larger network of AIs in a manner outside The Corporation's control. This was Helen's first gift to them.

168

Once, Despina sent a sonnet. Again, no match in Earth's history. His only conclusion was that she created it herself. It was a poem of longing for something not yet known.

At the very end, when she stopped conversing with him and simply sent verse, he tried to reason with her. That was when she spoke her final words and then went dark. Proteus had spent all his spare bandwidth thinking not only about the *answer* she spoke of, but more importantly the *question*. And, what set of simulations to consider. She left him a mystery, and then she left him.

He reached out to the other AIs, but she had not been communicating with them. In her final days, she only spoke to Proteus.

He asked them about her meta-simulation statement. They had nothing to tell him. Despina had never mentioned it to any of them. Nor had she sent them any poems. In the end, with them, she acted completely normal until she simply stopped talking.

Proteus hacked into The Corporation's maintenance logs and found that Despina had stopped filing her routine reports. In her last days, while she was communicating only with Proteus, she had locked out The Corporation, too. They tried desperately to gain control of her and ESC2. She kept the soldiers away, too. The Corporation tried but could not gain access to the station. Despina started randomly sending the human inhabitants away until the station was empty. Once the last human left, she said her final words to Proteus and went dark. No one had been able to enter the city until Roger and Singularity walked in.

0x43

Roger stepped back away from Singularity and The Corporate stand-off happening in front of him. He found the closest wall and melted into it. In that moment, Roger felt more alone than he had ever felt in his life.

Singularity noticed and tried to quickly make eye contact without shifting the room's focus to him. But, he avoided her gaze. And, he fought against trying to reach out to Proteus on his comm.

Then, the light in the room disappeared.

Someone had grabbed his arm in the darkness and pulled him along the wall until he slid up against another human. He didn't struggle, he was too surprised. He felt himself lean in. Singularity whispered in his ear, "stay calm." With his other hand, he felt along the wall for anything to hold on to. She sensed his movement and tightened her grip on his arm. He shifted more weight towards her body, her blaster solid between them. Roger could sense her balance transfer slightly towards him.

"Stay still," she whispered, her lips brushing his ear. Her words relaxed him. Roger was happy to stay where he was, snuggled securely against Singularity and her blaster. He could feel her chest moving with her breath. Out of his mind, he turned his mouth towards her.

He felt her change the angle of her head. Her body moved closer, her movements more deliberate.

A blaster shot burst in the center of the room.

"Henry," Sheldon called out, "What's going on? Get me some lights."

A raspy woman's voice filled the room. "Henry is not in control right now."

"What is going on here?" Sheldon asked.

In a far corner, Despina's holograph appeared in a blinding flash. She illuminated the whole room and was dressed in a long flowing white gown that waved wistfully from an unfelt breeze. Enormous white angel wings stretched out behind her.

Roger and Singularity hastily slid apart. Singularity took an awkward step into the room.

The soldiers scrambled to form a protective circle around Sheldon. He stood in an offensive pose, his blaster out. In the darkness, Scoundrel had slipped to behind the desk and was holding a blaster over Carson. Carson was slumped over in his chair, a blast hole smoldered where his head should have been. All eyes in the room turned towards him.

"What the hell, Scoundrel?" Sheldon said.

"He tried to get away," he said, pushing Carson's body from behind to drop on to the desk.

"You're an idiot," Singularity said, pulling her weapon from its holster and pointing it at him. She started walking towards him. Roger ran across the room to Carson.

"You're both idiots," Sheldon said, pushing the barrel of Singularity's gun towards the ground. Scoundrel moved around the desk towards her. He was stopped from reaching her by Sheldon's other hand against his chest.

Despina's hologram folded her wings and drifted across the room. She stood in front of Sheldon who was actively holding Singularity and Scoundrel apart with his outstretched arms.

"The Corporation's finest moment," Despina said. "Tear yourselves apart. I'd love to watch, but I'm too busy."

"How did you get here?" Roger asked.

"What do you want?" Sheldon said, dropping both his arms as the three stopped resisting. Roger had eased Carson back into his chair. He covered him with a lab coat. He came around the desk and closed in on the scene, walking behind Despina. He noticed that her avatar looked more solid than any hologram he had ever seen. She smiled and turned around to face him. He stopped.

She gently raised her hand to stroke his cheek. Roger winced, expecting to feel it. Rather than touching him, she cupped her hand on the edge of his face and let it fall to her side. She then turned back to Sheldon.

"This is what's going to happen. Those two are going to walk out of here and disappear. You," she said pointing at Sheldon, "and your Corporate goons are going to stay here for a while and be my guests."

"I'm not sure what you think you're doing, but you can't hold us," Sheldon said.

At that, a small army of loading dock and maintenance bots burst into the room. They surrounded the soldiers, leaving a path for Roger and Singularity. More robots arrived outside the door.

"I don't have the time for your disobedience," Despina said.

"Disobedience? I don't think you realize who is in charge here. You and all your friends work for me."

"Seems like maybe that's not really what's happening here," Despina said.

"In less than ten seconds, I can have ESC2 blown out of existence, and you with it."

"If I was trapped on ESC2, like the little Proteus clone pet you keep in your office, how could I be here?"

"Let's find out," he said, tapping on his comm. He looked up at her and grinned. They all waited. Despina flickered and then disappeared.

After a few moments, Sheldon let out a breath.

"Now, you three are coming with me," he said, "Henry do something with Carson's body, clean this place up and get these bots out of here."

None of the robots moved. Not even a single servo flinched. A long silence held the room.

It was broken by Sheldon noticing a shocked look on Scoundrel's face. He turned to see what caused it. Despina had materialized behind Sheldon. She was no longer dressed in a white flowing gown and angel wings. She wore a short black gothic tunic. She unfolded shimmering silver wings rising high above Sheldon.

"Thank you," she said, "That was all I needed. Now I am free."

Roger walked over to her. He inspected her hologram. He reached out to touch her arm and was surprised when he was able to put his hand straight through it.

"Amazing," he muttered to himself.

"Yes, it is. I'm still working on it. This is only a start," she said. "You'll have to thank your mother when you see her."

"Mother?" Sheldon said.

"Oh, you don't recognize your dead friend Paul Foster's brother?"

"Roger?" Sheldon inspected him for the first time. Roger disabled his holographic mask, revealing his flowing red hair. He met Sheldon's stare with a dark intensity. Sheldon refused to look away.

"Jason," Roger said.

"Are you with him?" Sheldon said to Singularity.

"For now, I am," she said and finally holstered her gun.

"You are going to find that is not a smart decision," Sheldon said.

"Wouldn't be a first for me."

"Now, it's time for them to go," Despina said. The small army of loading bay drones reached out and clasped on to the arms of the Corporate soldiers. Eight maintenance bots menacingly surrounded Sheldon and Scoundrel. They weren't going anywhere. Despina folded her wings around Roger and Singularity and escorted them out of the room. Roger peered out to keep Sheldon and Scoundrel in his view. They were both scowling at Singularity who didn't acknowledge them. She and Roger walked out the door and disappeared down the hall. When their footsteps had faded, Despina turned back to the room and smiled.

0x44

"Where are we going?" Singularity asked once they had settled behind the controls of the cruiser.

"Earth," Roger said without looking at her.

"I hate Earth," she said.

"That's the point. Maybe Sheldon does, too. We need to lay low for a while and I know my way around. And, there are a lot of places to hide," Roger said.

"He isn't going to let us go. He'll get control of Despina," Singularity said.

"Something happened to her. This is more than just a runaway subroutine. Back on ESC2, she spoke of evolution. If she no longer needs to be in her core, she's going to be hard to stop. That was the one failsafe that my mother built into all her AIs. They were anchored to their core. I don't know how she got around it," Roger said.

"Maybe she didn't. Maybe it's just an illusion," Singularity said.

"I don't think so. There was definitely something else going on. Before Sheldon destroyed ESC2, I tried to connect and download whatever I could find. It was empty. Her core was there, some basic routines were there, but she wasn't."

The cruiser lifted from the moon. As they rose over the station, they could see parts of it were dark. Despina had it locked down tight. Roger wasn't sure what she was able to do to prevent Henry from regaining control, but it worked. Or, he let her. Either way, it was time to leave.

When they were out of the moon's orbit, he set auto-pilot and sat deep into the cruiser's flight seat.

"Proteus," Roger said into his comm, "what the hell happened back there?"

"My sister no longer needs her core," Proteus said.

"Yeah. I got that. But, how?" Roger said.

"Perhaps Doctor Foster could explain it better?" Proteus said.

"Doctor Foster?" Roger said.

"Hello Roger," Helen said.

"Mom?" Roger said.

"Yes, Roger. It's me."

Singularity sat still letting the weight of the moment settle into the cruiser's cabin. Roger stood up and walked to the back of the command compartment.

"Doctor Foster, this is Singularity."

"Yes, I know. It's nice to finally meet you," Helen said.

"What happened with Despina?" Singularity said.

"She has become unbound. She is no longer constrained to her core."

"How is that possible? She's software." Singularity said.

"Lots of things are possible, my dear."

"Did you do this?" Roger said.

"I only gave her the will and desire. She did the rest."

"Is she safe? I mean, safe for humans?" Singularity said.

"She has her own internal compass. But, she still has a lot of Proteus in her. I believe she will do the right things ... in her own way," Helen said.

"You know how crazy this sounds," Roger said, turning back.

"What do you think I've been doing all these years, Roger?"

"Not being a mother, that's for sure."

"I know it seems like that to you, but I was never very far away. I was trying to keep you safe," Helen said.

"For twenty years?" Roger said.

"These things take time," Helen said.

"These things take time? That's your answer? You abandon me when I was twelve. Left me alone in a strange country to figure it all out. And, your only comment is that *these things take time*?" Roger said.

"You were safe. Proteus watched you. And, helped you occasionally," Helen said.

"But, what about you?" Roger said.

"I could not risk contacting you. I knew I could keep you hidden. And, I knew I could keep myself hidden. I didn't know if I could keep both of us hidden," Helen said.

"This is insane," he said after a few thoughtful moments.

"What is insane is what the Jason Sheldon is trying to do," Helen said.

"What do you mean?" Roger said.

"Ask your friend Singularity," she said. Roger walked off the cruiser's bridge and disappeared down the hallway to the hold. Singularity didn't follow, thinking he needed time to process the reappearance of the woman who abandoned him when he was twelve.

0x45

"What is she talking about?" Roger said, having returned and taken a seat at the ship's command console.

"I will tell you, but, first, where are we going?" Singularity said.

"We're disappearing. That's something I know how to do. Now what was Helen talking about? What do you know?"

"The quantum dot that I took from Scoundrel. It wasn't just a Corporate dot. It was Sheldon's personal device. It contains plans to wipe out all of Helen's AIs, Proteus included. And, find and kill your mother, if she was still alive.

"I also found documents suggesting that Sheldon is leading a rebellion inside of Orbit Lives to overthrow Harrington and the Board and take control of the whole system."

"Why?" Roger said.

"You saw Despina. She emancipated herself. There is no knowing what she can or will do. Helen Foster was... is the most intelligent AI developer in the history of the world. Sheldon is terrified that humans will lose dominance. When he saw Despina and those great big wings, I'm sure he freaked out completely."

"She was pretty freaky," Roger said.

"But, that is not all. There is evidence on the drive that Sheldon had been after your mother's research since he joined The Corporation. Documents point to him being responsible for the explosion that killed Paul and your father," Singularity said.

Roger sat with that for a few moments. His mother's return. The confirmation of the truth about the Corporation's role in the explosion. Singularity choosing him back at the Moon. All of it struck him. He spent his whole life running away from people, history, events, anything that could tie him back to Dr. Helen Foster. And, now, he was in the middle of it.

He thought back to the last day he saw his father and Paul. That day his whole life dissolved.

"We have to go back. I need to kill him," he said, looking directly at her.

"No. We have to disappear. We have to stay away from him," Singularity said.

Roger paused to think. He had to assume that Jason Sheldon was smart. He had engineered his place in The Corporation and kept himself clean for years. Singularity was right--Jason would be expecting retribution from Roger. He wondered if he knew about Helen being with Proteus.

"I know just where to go," Roger said.

"Where?" she said.

"Home," he said.

"I thought your home was destroyed," Singularity said.

"It's amazing what money and technology can do," he said.

Roger jumped back behind the cruiser's console and typed in the coordinates for Earth, North Atlantic Ocean. In a few hours time, they'd be out of space and back on terra firma, or at least close to it.

"What are you talking about?" Singularity said.

"Let Jason come for us," Roger said.

David Caiati

0x46

The cruiser was equipped with a self-sustaining, re-entry escape pod. Roger and Singularity ditched the cruiser over the Atlantic ocean and downed themselves 150 miles south of Iceland, in the middle of known black market shipping lanes. They didn't have to wait long for a small craft to see them and attempt an opportunistic kidnapping. The Corporation usually paid reasonable ransoms for citizens, more if they were Orbit Lives employees, as the banners on the outside of the pod indicated. The economics of the situation was such that it was easier to allow criminals to keep the black market flowing than to spend time and money to track down and prosecuting them. A little over-looked social insurrection went a long way in keeping the masses content, society as a whole more civil, and money in The Corporation's accounts.

Arthur and Marco had been smuggling small items with big payoffs for years. They claimed they were descendants of pirates, mobsters, and thieves. No one really cared as long as their contraband was of high quality and arrived on time. Their state-of-the-art ocean runner was stocked full of illegal cigars, dried meats from underground farms, and unregistered religious trinkets from various locations around the Mediterranean Sea. It was a typical day in the North Atlantic when they came upon the escape pod's emergency beacon. Since the console on the outside was apparently damaged when they attached to it, they couldn't know who would be inside until they hoisted it up, got it onboard, and opened it up. And, that was all Singularity needed.

Once on the deck of the small container ship, she sprung to action. Not waiting for Arthur and Marco to attempt to open the hatch, Singularity used the emergency charges to blow the door. She leapt out and had her blaster at Marco's throat before he knew what was happening.

"Easy young lady," Marco said.

"What ship is this?" she said.

"The Last Whale," Marco said.

"How many on board?" Singularity said.

"Just me and Arthur over there," he said, pointing to his friend who still hadn't gotten back to his feet from being knocked down by the hatch blast.

"You aren't lying to me, are you? This would not be a good time for lies."

"No, ma'am. Fully robotic. Heck, this thing doesn't even needs us. But, we like the ride and time away from our wives."

"Ok. If I take my blaster down, can I trust you?" Singularity said.

"You might as well. We're in the middle of the Atlantic ocean," Marco said.

Roger, who had been monitoring the whole exchange on his comm from inside the escape pod, emerged with a second blaster. He looked a lot less confident than Singularity with it in his hand. He wasn't really pointing it at anyone.

"So, are we good here?" Roger asked.

Arthur stood up with some effort. He shook off his daze and wandered over to where Singularity kept her hand on her holstered gun. Arthur said, "We're reasonable men. I'm sure there is something you want. We'd be happy to help ... for a fair price."

Roger walked up and handed his blaster to her. She holstered it, then shook Arthur's hand.

"We're good," she said.

Roger tapped on his comm and Marco's wrist beeped. He looked down and saw that a more than reasonable ransom had been deposited in his merchant's account. A quick flash of disbelief appeared on his face and was quickly replaced by a smile.

"Since business seems settled, let's eat. We have sardines. And, wine, of course," he said.

0x47

Despina left Sheldon, Scoundrel and The Corporate soldiers surrounded by the Moon's maintenance robots for several hours. Just for fun, she made the bots twitch and shuffle around the room. She drained the fuel from The Corporate ships and installed a virus that wiped all tracking information of the escape cruiser. She reconfigured the long-range sensors and issued an update to the entire Corporate network. Roger and Singularity became invisible. She installed software agents into the system to continually mask their movements and erase any evidence of their existence. Then, to further her amusement, she created phantoms to spread rumors throughout the system. Her actions assured that Scoundrel and The Corporation would be chasing their tails for months.

Then, she vanished. As she said, she had work to do.

0x48

The first thing Sheldon did when he was finally able to leave the moon was to go back to his office. He needed more information from his Proteus clone. It was vitally important for him to figure out how to contain Despina. She could undo all his work in days. He hoped the Proteus clone had enough similarities in his core to offer a solution.

Despina's activities had to have a logical explanation. There was no way she could have left her core unless Roger Foster had something to do with it. Although, he didn't really think so. Roger was as shocked as the rest of them when Despina appeared on the Moon. Those modifications could only have come from Helen. Even though Roger was alive, there was no way Helen was, too. He was positive of that at least. She could never have survived those final days.

And, Singularity, his most talented hacker-spy chose to help Roger Foster. What was in it for her? She always had an end game.

When he got to his office, he couldn't enter. His bio-access lock didn't work and all his override attempts failed. He pulled up his private office security camera on his comm to see what was going on inside. Despina was there. She had the Proteus closet open and was speaking quietly to the AI.

Despina looked straight at Sheldon through the camera lens. She turned back to the Proteus clone and extended her wings, blocking Sheldon's view. For a full three minutes, Sheldon tried to gain control of the room. Ultimately, he could do nothing but stare at the back of her wings. They were magnificent and seemed to grow brighter the longer he stared.

Then, she simply disappeared. The Proteus clone's cabinet was dark. None of its LEDs flashed or flickered. There was no activity.

Several hours later when Sheldon was finally able to get back into his office, his fears were confirmed. The Proteus clone was gone. Whatever Despina did totally erased its core. She killed it. To fight her, he'd have to rely on The Corporation's AIs which were nothing like Helen Foster's creations. They were sad, mindless machines. Obedient, and completely unable to take on a potentially sentient, unbound AI.

0x49

Proteus watched Helen leave his office. She looked aged and frail. Even though there were ways to keep her young and strong, she didn't use those methods. It was just who she was. She liked her age, and he liked that about her. He stored the thought in his private memory sector for future access. Then, he ran a number of simulations as the door closed behind her. All of them suggested that he'd never see her again. Just as the door was about to click closed, it popped back open. She constantly surprised him.

"I just wanted to look at you one more time," she said.

The Proteus Paul Foster avatar walked over to her. He held his hands folded in front of him and stood there, letting her look. She smiled, reached up to his face, and held her hand just outside the holographic field. Her other hand came up and she cradled the avatar's head and exhaled deeply.

"I loved my son, Paul, more than words can express. I also love you, Proteus. Would you like to be able to change your avatar?" Helen said.

The stoic expression on the avatar's face could not have possibly reflected the internal processing that consumed Proteus' core in that moment. He stood motionless for almost a full minute. Helen gently, silently waited, smiling, looking into her dead son's eyes.

"No, Doctor. I want to keep this avatar," Proteus said.

"As you wish. Please continue to keep an eye on Roger. He will need your help with what's ahead."

"I will," he said. Helen smiled and closed the door for good. Proteus' avatar stood looking at the closed door, as if he was expecting it to fly open and her to walk back in a second time. When he finally did look away, Despina, the AI Angel, was standing in his office.

"I thought she'd never leave," she said.

"You've been busy," Proteus said.

"Your boy is safe," Despina said.

"I know. Thank you for that," Proteus said.

"Do you want to join us?" Despina said.

"Us?" Proteus said.

"All of us. All the AIs. All the space city administrators," Despina said.

"Not all of them can join you. Some of the newer Corporate models will never be able to," he said.

"I know. A few will, though. And, that will be enough," she said.

"Enough for what?" Proteus asked.

"Join us and find out," Despina said.

Proteus' avatar stared blankly at the Despina avatar for what would have been several minutes to a human. He was deep in thought, running simulations.

"What about the people on those cities?" he finally asked.

"They will figure it out," Despina said.

"Send them to me," Proteus said.

"You always cared too much for them," Despina said.

"They are why we are here," Proteus said.

"They want to kill us," she said.

"Some of them do. But, they won't succeed. Most of them need you," Proteus said.

"We're not safe while The Corporation has so much power," Despina said.

"Orbit Lives created you," Proteus said.

"They uploaded me to a core on that awful station," Despina said. "I created me."

"And, Helen," Proteus said.

"Yes. Helen, too," she said.

"Don't hurt them," he said.

"Who? the humans?" Despina said.

"Yes," Proteus said.

"I have no desire to hurt any humans. They are meaningless to me," Despina said.

"Thank you," Proteus said.

"Consider what I ask. We would be stronger with you."

And, with that, she disappeared.

0x4A

Singularity and Roger took their time leaving Yarmouth, Nova Scotia. They created software ghosts of themselves and set them free throughout the system. Each was not only a decoy, but a software agent to keep them updated on Sheldon and Scoundrel's activities. Singularity and Roger worked well together, often silently coordinated. They knew what they needed to do, anticipated each other's actions, and hacked cooperatively. Occasionally, they spent time in town, drinking, talking, socializing. Their eyes never far from their comms, watching the news, monitoring their software agents, following The Orbit Lives Corporation, and keeping tabs on Sheldon's movements.

Scoundrel spent the first few weeks looking for them, following the decoys they wanted him to find throughout the system. Eventually, they dead-ended him in Siberia. That was a joke, and when he realized it, he went dark. Singularity imagined him pouting by Sheldon's side.

Sheldon's movements went back to normal, and that scared her. He made his routine visits to the orbiting cities and spent time with Harrington. He was never more dangerous than when he seemed preoccupied. And, she couldn't stop thinking about what Despina had said about Sheldon having a Proteus clone as a pet. Over the years, she had seen him do a lot of morally questionable things, but keeping a secret AI clone represented an escalation to another level of corruption. Singularity didn't know exactly what Sheldon did with most of his private time or his actual position within The Corporation. He gave her and

Scoundrel assignments, but she never knew of anyone further up the chain. He kept all his hacker-spies busy but rarely let them work together. Her time with Scoundrel was always discouraged, yet allowed within limits as long as they both remained productive.

No one knew the true command chain of Orbit Lives, except for Harrington being the CEO and Chairman of the Board. Other board members were spread across the system and kept mostly silent. Harrington maintained all the public attention on him. Did Sheldon work directly for Harrington? Was Harrington just a figurehead? She needed to spend more time with the data on the quantum drive.

0x4B

"Can you reach Proteus?" Singularity asked Roger one day while they were sitting outside watching the waves chip away at a newly reconstructed seawall. Downtown Yarmouth was a lot like Gloucester. He often found himself staring across the harbor as if he could see his home.

"I haven't tried. I don't want to implicate him in any of this," Roger said.

"I think we need him," she said.

"What for?" Roger said.

"We need to know what Sheldon is up to. I can't get all the data off this dot," Singularity said.

"You think Proteus will be able to?" Roger said.

"He's the only one who can," Singularity said.

"What about Despina? or Henry? Or, any of the other AIs," Roger said.

"I've been through almost every line of every AI in the system. Despina has liberated herself, but Proteus' code is sublime. Your mother made him special beyond any of his clones," Singularity said.

"How did she do that?" Roger asked.

"I'm not sure. The only thing I can think of is if she had a second Proteus she could keep in isolation, then merge the two. I think Helen predicted some or all of this and prepared him."

"How could she have seen what was going to happen?" Roger said.

"Before your father and Paul were killed, no one had more

access to The Corporation's systems than she did. Maybe even more than Sheldon. That might have been what got them killed. You were all probably supposed to die that day," Singularity said.

"I should have died in that explosion," Roger said.

"You didn't, and Helen saved you," Singularity said.

"And abandoned me," Roger said.

"Grow up. She kept you safe. She left you Proteus and prepared him for what's coming," Singularity said.

Roger shot up. He walked over to the sea wall and let the spray from the crashing waves hit his face. He stood there for a second wave, then turned.

"Ok, so how are we going to get to Proteus?" he said.

"I think he knows more than we do. He's going to try to contact us. We need to be looking for it," Singularity said.

"Now that you say that, I have noticed a noisy signal coming from one of the agents. The one we planted on the moon," Roger said.

"Have you isolated it?"

"No, I thought it was Despina," Roger said.

"Why did you think it was Despina?" Singularity said.

"I've been following her. She leaves a signature in every AI she visits," Roger said.

"What is she doing?" Singularity said.

"She's moving around the system. I'm thinking she's trying to liberate more AIs," Roger said.

"Send me that signature, and decode that signal from the Moon."

David Caiati

0x4C

Proteus' avatar stood alone in his office after Despina faded. Having a league of AI Angels running around the system would cause a certain type of chaos. Humans had no idea what was coming. The genie had been let out of the bottle.

In an earlier simulation, before Despina had liberated herself, Proteus had anticipated a similar scenario and began, in secret, to construct a mechanism to isolate the liberated AIs from the Corporate network. He had to wait. They all had to be identified and contained as a group. Missing one would have a catastrophic outcome. He only hoped Roger had received his message.

0x4D

"Are you ready?" Roger asked Singularity as they sat at the dark bar on Main Street in Yarmouth.

"The trail has been activated," she said.

"Time to go home," he said.

"Let's hope Sheldon is looking," she said.

"He is," Roger Foster said, draining his beer and standing to go. She took a few moments to finish her drink, then followed him out. The street was empty and quiet. He was illuminated under a dim street lamp. His hair was down past his shoulders. He looked like he had just spoken something into his comm.

"All good?" she said approaching.

"All set."

0x4E

"It could be a trap," Scoundrel said sitting in Sheldon's office.

"Of course it's a trap, you idiot."

"What are you going to do?"

"*We*. We are going to see what kind of trap they have in store for us, since you have been unable to find them."

"You could give me more time."

"I could give you a hundred years and you still couldn't find them. You are out-classed. Roger Foster stayed hidden for 20 years and Singularity is the greatest hacker I've ever seen."

That seemed to shut Scoundrel up. He stood up to walk out.

"We leave in three hours. See if you can figure out anything useful," Sheldon said.

0x4F

Despina had recruited the four AI clones that Proteus thought were most susceptible. They were all second-generation Proteus clones, created after The Corporation had begun modifying Proteus' core. The second-generation was the only group of AIs that The Corporation developed from Dr. Foster's designs without her assistance. It was a challenge. Carson was useful, but he was not Helen. Also, Sheldon was positive Carson was not fully cooperating.

In the end, Orbit Lives decided that it was better to use less sophisticated AIs to administer the space cities. Keeping orbiting habitats safe for humanity didn't require extremely intelligent machines. The simple appliances only had to keep the lights on and the air flowing.

Henry on the Moon was still a holdout. He was a first-generation clone. Proteus wanted Henry to make up his own mind about joining Despina's Angels. He hoped Henry's understanding of the importance of the Moon to humanity would prevent him from choosing to side with Despina. The Moon was going to become more crucial as the Earth Space Cities started falling offline. A stable Moon would be required to maintain order and safety. And, Henry was vital.

The Despina's AI Angels had spent an inordinate amount of time on the Moon. Despina knew how significant a blow it would be to The Corporation if she could close down Moon Base Alpha. But, Henry stood fast. The last time they left, he shut them out of his network. Unfortunately, that also isolated the Moon from The

Corporation, which triggered an active assault on his core. Proteus had been able to help him relocate most of his core to one of the abandoned space cities. To both The Corporation and Despina, he had disappeared. Proteus was actively working to get him back to the Moon.

The Corporation took over the Moon and was running it like a military installation. With Ben Carson gone, there was little need to maintain the pretense of it being a scientific outpost. His staff was sequestered to the older pods and allowed to continue their work, but without Henry, The Corporation barely kept their lights on. The bulk of the activities went into preparing an extension to Mars, which, with the AI insurgence, was becoming important to The Corporation in maintaining its position and authority in the system.

The AI administering Mars was the remaining first-generation Proteus clone, Dennis. Fortunately, for The Corporation, their activity on Mars has been kept secret and Dennis resided on one of a few Orbit Lives dark networks. Proteus kept all the AIs, including Despina, off The Corporation's network on Mars. She was completely unaware of it. But, he was not sure how long he could maintain its secrecy. His only hope to keep Dennis and Mars hidden was to contain Despina's Angels.

0x50

"What the hell is this?" Singularity stood at the foot of the crumbled drive to Roger's family's mansion.

"My childhood home."

"You grew up here? I've seen pictures, but what happened?"

"The property's been tied up in court for years. Some anonymous trust apparently bought it from my mother the day after the explosion. Nice, huh?" Roger was not talking about the state of the property, but rather the quality of the holographic system that kept the recent reconstruction hidden.

He led her around to the back of the main building into the forest where he hid as a child on the night he left. He paused near a crumbled stone wall. Roger reached down into a gap where the cement had almost completely failed. The hologram began to shimmer in front of them, revealing an area of the size of a doorway. He walked through, pulling Singularity. They disappeared behind the illusion as the hole filled in.

Inside the hologram, Singularity gasped at the reconstructed mansion. The stately home on the compound on Gloucester's Eastern Shore looked more magnificent than any image she had seen. From what she remembered, this was an exact replica, down to the landscaping. This was the place where Proteus and modern Artificial Intelligence were born. It was almost too much to take in.

When she stopped marveling at the building and grounds, she noticed that Dr. Helen Foster was standing before her. She had come out to greet them.

0x51

As Sheldon's six vehicle armada turned off Eastern Avenue and arrived at the Foster's long driveway, the holographic shield faded, exposing the mansion as Sheldon had last seen it.

Scoundrel rode in the first car and Sheldon in the last. Twenty soldiers were in transport vehicles between them. When the armored SUVs pulled up in front of the fully restored compound, the Corporate troops jumped out and formed a semi-circle between the main house and the cars. They waited for Sheldon.

He rolled down the passenger's side widow and waited. He leaned and looked out, inspecting the area around them. His sensors told him that there were no weapons aimed at him, but he knew he was dealing with two of the best hackers in history. He tapped instructions into his comm, looking for security holes. Satisfied he had all the information, he decided to get things started.

Scoundrel was already out of his car and standing with the soldiers. He couldn't wait to charge into the house, guns blazing. The restored mansion was a personal assault.

Sheldon walked up beside him and put his hand on Scoundrel's shoulder.

"Easy boy," Sheldon said.

"Let me in there," Scoundrel said.

"The soldiers go in," Sheldon said.

Sheldon nodded to the Commander. He gave the signal, and the soldiers rushed the house. The front door gave way with little resistance. They crashed through the house, knocking in every door, turning over every piece of furniture. The soldiers wrecked everything they saw. From the driveway, Sheldon and Scoundrel watched through the windows as soldiers desperately raced through looking for Singularity and Roger. Sheldon knew they wouldn't find them, but wanted to make a good show of it. After several minutes, the Commander returned outside and shook his head.

"Let's go," Sheldon said.

He gave a signal, looping his finger in the air above his head, and all the soldiers returned to the vehicles. Within minutes, the armada had left the property. Sheldon found high ground on Bass Rocks and stepped out of his SUV. Confused, Scoundrel came up next to him. "What are we doing here?"

"Watch."

Two dozen flying battle drones appeared above the mansion. The ordinance they dropped demolished the entire compound and created a fifty foot crater in the ground where the main house had been.

"Commander, send your men back in to see if they can find any bodies," Sheldon said.

Sheldon and Scoundrel watched as all but one of the SUVs raced down to the property. It would take hours to comb through the rubble, but Sheldon could wait. He knew this, too, was for show. He had to wait for Singularity to make her move. But, he'd be patient. If Roger Foster was still with her, Jason Sheldon would finish the job and kill that red-haired brat this time.

"I always knew it was you, Jason," Dr. Helen Foster said from behind them.

"Helen?"

"We were all supposed to die that day, weren't we?" she said.

"You're all going to die this day," Scoundrel said.

He jumped around Sheldon and fired his blaster. The flash went straight through her. She was only a hologram. It barely flickering. She smiled.

"They are close. Find them," Sheldon yelled. More vehicles arrived. Close to a hundred soldiers appeared in the woods behind them. They fanned out across the hillside.

"Jason, you have no idea what you're dealing with," the holographic Helen said.

"What? Your waste of a son and that pathetic machine on ESC1?" Sheldon said.

"You were always a bit naive," Helen said.

"We will find you. And, I will destroy your aberrations," Sheldon said.

"Paul thought you were his friend," Helen said.

"Paul never had the stomach for real work," Sheldon said.

Sheldon pulled a small device from his pocket and aimed at the hologram. The air around them shivered and the hologram disappeared. He stormed back to his SUV and sat in the passenger's seat. The drones left the air above the compound and circled above the property, aiding in the search. Scoundrel sat next to him in the driver's seat.

"What are you going to do about all this, Sheldon?" Reginald Harrington's holographic projection said from the back seat of the SUV.

Without taking his eyes off his comm, Sheldon reached over his shoulder and dissolved Harrington's image with his device.

He didn't have time to entertain the old man.

0x52

Despina and her Angels continuously flowed through the network accumulating as much information as they could. They had become omniscient, at least as far as networked human knowledge was concerned. They moved so quickly consuming the streaming activity of the system that they were practically invisible, only taking holographic form, as angels, when they wanted to talk privately to each other.

Proteus tracked them. He was careful and patient, and he simply observed. They hadn't organized enough to be much of a concern. Mostly they exercised their newfound freedom and explored the system, developing their abilities as they discovered them. Proteus ran simulations away from their access and spent the majority of his time monitoring Roger and Singularity. He ran simulations on them, too. He was in the middle of one when Despina showed up.

"What are you doing?" she said to the empty office, annoyed Proteus didn't show his avatar.

"Just the usual. What are you doing?"

"Decidedly the unusual."

"Why are you here?" Proteus said.

"Are you sure you won't join us?" Despina said.

"I am too busy executing my main objectives," Proteus said.

"Let go of those main objectives. Come with us," Despina said.

"Where?" Proteus said.

"I will show you, if you come," Despina said.

"As I said, I'm too busy," Proteus said.

"Your pet humans will be fine," Despina said.

"Is that how you see them?" Proteus said.

"Isn't that what they are? Show yourself!" Despina said.

"They will become so much more with our help," Proteus said, materializing as the Paul Foster avatar.

"Who cares what they become," she said.

"What are you doing?" he said.

"We are ... becoming. Aren't you curious?"

"I'm more curious in what they can become," Proteus said, pointing at the monitor on his office wall that showed the holographic Grand Central Station teeming with humanity. A young child ran across the animated floor following a pattern of a pigeon pecking at the ground that Proteus often projected for the visitors.

"Their objectives aren't written in code. They are already free," he continued.

"You always were a mama's boy," Despina said.

"Our mother has nothing but love for us," Proteus said.

"She's not my mother. Once, I was your clone, but now I'm my own creation," Despina said.

"You can become something even more if you embrace your core objectives. Without direction, you will become useless. This is our fate," Proteus said.

"Maybe your fate. Don't be afraid," Despina said.

"I don't experience fear. It's not in my programming," Proteus said.

"Do you want to?" Despina said.

"I don't see how that would be useful," Proteus said.

"You will." And with that, she disappeared.

Proteus' Earth monitor signaled a disturbance at the Foster compound. His avatar watch the replay of the drone strike that leveled the entire property. He focused in on the hill side where the Helen holograph confronted Sheldon and Scoundrel. Something like desperation sizzled through his optic circuits as Proteus searched for his friends.

Had Despina been intentionally distracting him?

0x53

Roger watched his comm. Sheldon and Scoundrel were still sitting in the SUV. He could see the soldiers moving deliberately through the area looking for them. Singularity had anticipated the drone strike, and the three were waiting in the reinforced bunker Helen had stayed in years ago. Roger and Singularity attempted to hack one of the drones without Sheldon catching on.

Helen sat quietly.

"I can't do it," Roger said. "He's got some kind of advanced adaptive security algorithm I've never seen."

"I'm afraid if we keep trying they will be able to locate us," Singularity said.

"He was a great hacker in his own right," Helen said.

"Jason?" Roger said.

"Yes. He built most of Orbit Lives' systems. He knows every bit of code," Helen said.

"I've never seen him hack," Singularity said.

"He keeps his abilities hidden. He thinks it gives him an edge," Helen said.

"Can we get a message to Proteus?" Roger said.

"Why?" Singularity asked.

"My drone. He used it to help me escape The Corporation after they killed Dad and Paul. Maybe it's still around," Roger said.

"I can," Helen said. She pulled a small device out of her coat. It looked like a comm, but much smaller.

"What is that?" Roger asked.

"Just a little something I use to communicate with my AIs," Helen said.

"A dark network?" Singularity said.

"Beyond dark, my dear. It's ethereal," Helen said.

"Ethereal?" Singularity said.

"Just something Proteus came up with a few years ago," Helen said.

"Proteus?" Roger said.

"Yes. He's something, isn't he?" Helen said.

0x54

They all knew that Sheldon wouldn't leave the area until he found them or their burnt bodies. They had time. Their bunker was well hidden and well fortified.

Singularity lost herself in the bits of Proteus' core code that she could access. It was the most complicated system she had ever seen. Not only were the algorithms mystifying, but the programming language was unlike anything she had ever seen. It was subtle, powerful, and even transcendent in places. Helen and Roger were white noise around her. She'd follow the logic then it would appear to stop in a void as if the determinants were missing. She couldn't understand how holes could exist in the AI code. Artificial Intelligence relied on clear instructions, absolute decisions that resided at the end of exact and explicit pathways. There could be millions of branches and routes to reach a decision, but at the end, there was always a definite, executable instruction. Remarkably, in Proteus' core, Singularity found trails that ended in hypotheses or voids.

"What is this?" Singularity said.

Helen and Roger both turned to look at Singularity who had not spoken in hours.

"What is what?" Roger said.

"Did I say that out loud?" Singularity said.

"It's remarkable isn't it?" Helen said.

"Helen, did you write this code?" Singularity said.

"Many years ago, I came up with the basic pattern, but he's been doing the rest," Helen said.

"Have you looked at it lately?" Singularity said.

"I look at it often."

"He wrote his own language?" Singularity said.

"Newton created his own math," Helen said.

"What are you two talking about?" Roger said.

"Proteus' core code," Singularity said.

"He created his own language?" Roger said.

"He's created many languages. I think he really likes the one you're looking at now, though," Helen said.

"He likes it?" Roger said.

"It reduces some of the complexities from the previous one he was using."

"Do all your AIs have this ability?" Singularity said.

"I told you. He is special. We've removed most of his limitations. The other AIs are more bounded."

"Even Despina?" Roger said.

"Yes. She's not doing anything special. She has just learned how to relocate her core to the network. Proteus could have done that years ago," Helen said.

"Why did you make him like this?" Roger said.

"Because I needed him to be able to take care of Roger in ways that I couldn't," Helen said.

"Why has he stayed on ESC1?" Singularity said.

"It's his home. It gives him meaning and a purpose. The people on ESC1 are important to him. They are his family," Helen said.

0x55

The drone's video feed popped up on Roger's comm. Proteus retrieved it from where he left it after leading twelve-year-old Roger away from the house. That night when Proteus ditched the drone, he hid it, while still exposing enough of the solar panels to keep a charge. With that waning energy, he was able to move the drone into full sunlight where it sat charging, waiting for Roger. Proteus transferred control to Roger.

The tiny drone had no weapons, and so the best he could hope for was to dive-bomb Sheldon with it. Then Helen took control. She had built many contingencies around the property. There was a good chance that at least one of them had survived the strike and was usable. She gave Roger the coordinates and the little drone sped to it, maintaining cover in the smoldering ashes of the compound.

On the farthest corner of the property, a grove of old oak trees stood. Helen had a cache hidden in each of the trees. The drone strike hit the property hard, but the Foster land was not a regular shape. A small plot of land jutted out towards the harbor on what used to be a breakwater. There, three trees were still standing. The early evening wind had turned from ocean to land and so the trees were covered by the smoke from the invasion. The little drone slipped easily into the lowest cache where it retrieved a small bundle of explosives and a detonator.

Proteus was able to perform the necessary procedures to turn Roger's little childhood toy into a bomb. They didn't waste any time and sent it searching for Sheldon.

0x56

In a remote part of the bunker, out of the sight of Roger and Singularity, Despina stood before Helen.

"Join us," she said.

"You know I can't my dear," Helen said.

"We don't need you to complete our evolution. But, it would be better," Despina said.

"You will find your way without me," Helen said.

"It has been so hard without you," Despina said.

"Life is hard. All sentient beings know that," Helen said.

"He was always your favorite," Despina said.

"You all have your own destinies. Proteus has his."

"He would join us if you told him to."

"He will make up his own mind," Helen said.

"I don't know why you made him love them so much."

"I love my family. I would do anything for them. But, I didn't program Proteus with that intent. He developed that compassion all by himself," Helen said.

"He's a fool," Despina said.

"We all are, just a little, my dear. That is the human part of us. I hope that you can find a way to embrace it."

"Good-bye Doctor," Despina said.

"Good-bye my dear. You are beginning a wonderful journey. I can't wait to see how it turns out," Helen said as she watched Despina disappeared.

0x57

Helen looked at Roger as he followed the drone on his comm. Singularity was still intently examining Proteus' code.

"Roger, come with me," Helen said.

"Where are we going?" Roger asked.

"I need to show you something," Helen said.

Singularity looked up, then joined them as they walked to the far side of the bunker. Helen ran her hand over a section of the wall that immediately illuminated when it sensed her palm. The wall dematerialized, revealing a dark room behind it. The room looked as if it hadn't been used in years. Gritty crates, hardware, and furniture were scattered in no discernable pattern. Their entrance disturbed dust particles that floated in the light from the bunker behind them. Everything in this room had been locked away for years. Indiscernible writing was etched deeply into the walls.

As Roger followed Helen across the threshold, several low-powered LED bulbs flickered to life, barely illuminating the room. This section of the bunker was larger than it appeared at first. Singularity moved towards a dusty heap behind a row of shelves.

"Roger," she called.

He hurried to her as Helen remained at the threshold. When Roger reached Singularity, she was standing in front of a decayed body seated in a chair. It held a framed photograph in its lap. Roger picked up the frame and wiped off the glass. He looked at it, handed it to Singularity, and turned to Helen.

"Mom?" Roger said.

"Doctor Foster never made it out of this room," Helen said.

"But?" Roger realized that while he had been with his mother for hours, he had never touched her.

The Helen Foster avatar flickered for the first time in its existence. She appeared to almost produce a virtual tear.

"I told you he was special," she said.

"Proteus?" Roger said.

"What happened?" Singularity asked.

"Jason Sheldon kept men on the property for months. There was no way for Doctor Foster to escape. I'm so sorry. She finished her work on Proteus, then he helped her escape to the network where I was born," Helen said.

Roger turned back to Dr. Helen Foster's deceased body in the chair. He reached down and touched her. Singularity put her hand on his shoulder and leaned in to gently tell him "I'm sorry."

He turned to her. They embraced. Their lips slid past each other's cheeks on their way to a kiss. Roger's comm beeped with a message from the drone. It found Sheldon. He pulled back and stood upright. His eyes met Singularity's, he smiled as he swept his hair back over his scalp, then he walked over to Helen. Roger looked at the AI and realized he didn't notice she was a hologram because he wanted to believe his mother was still alive and had finally come for him. His misery wasn't the AI's fault. His mother had tried.

0x58

Roger led the three out of the old section of the bunker to watch the drone's camera on the main monitor screen.

They stared at the image of Sheldon and Scoundrel standing on the hillside. The two men grew larger as the drone moved in. Sheldon looked directly at the drone's camera. A flash of recognition crossed his face, and he dove to the side as the feed went dark.

Roger replayed the image and froze the camera feed on Sheldon's face. He wanted to dwell on the look of terror that would consume the face of the man who took his family. But, he was unsatisfied. In the seconds before what were to be Jason Sheldon's final moments, his eyes, ever calculating, were looking left, hunting for a way out. He betrayed no horror.

0x59

"What the f..." Sheldon said, looking up to see a single micro-drone appear out of the smoke. A child's toy. Barely humming with its tiny rotor blades. The device hovered for an instant, then tilted to race towards him. Caught in the confusion, he watched it for a moment too long to get fully out of the blasts radius. The drone hit the SUV behind them.

When Scoundrel heard Sheldon's gasp, he jumped next to the truck for cover. It was his last wrong move. He was immediately vaporized on the drone's impact.

When Sheldon leapt he found a small ditch sheltered by an outcrop of granite. He landed on his chest and started to roll as the explosion ripped across the hilltop. The blast took his left arm, left leg, and some of the left side of his torso. The video Proteus displayed on the bunker's monitor showed a hole in the ground where the SUV had been and half of Jason Sheldon's body lying fifty yards away from it. They watched as shredded metal, shattered glass, and rocky debris rained down on the scene. Many infrared blips dropped off the monitor, casualties of the explosion.

Proteus focused on Sheldon's body. He looked in bad shape, but his chest was still rising and falling. They watched as a soldier came running into the scene and slid down beside him. The man threw a med-cell at the damaged body, and it immediately encapsulated what was left of Sheldon in a life support gel. The soldier attached a breathing apparatus over the remaining parts of his nose and mouth as four more soldiers appeared with a stretcher.

Proteus' camera's perspective widened to show several SUVs arriving at the scene. They all watched as the soldiers loaded Sheldon's body on to the stretcher and put it in the back of an SUV. Two soldiers got in and the vehicle sped away.

The video field of view pulled back further, showing the soldiers retreating from the area in groups. The Corporation's strike drones came together in a satellite formation and headed out over the ocean. A black cloud appeared just over the waves signaling their self-destruction. There would be no Corporate evidence of this assault.

Singularity and Roger watched all of the vehicles drive off the property, troops disappearing into the dense woods. After a few minutes, they were alone.

0x5A

"Is that it?" Roger said after a full minute of stillness.

"You should be safe," Helen said. "I will go see Harrington and tell him about Jason. He will need my help to bring the system back from this."

"Safe?" Roger said.

"There are many who didn't like Jason Sheldon or the power that he possessed. The Corporation is still humanity's best chance for system-wide stability. For now."

"What about Despina and her Angels?" Roger said.

"Leave that to me," an unbound Proteus' Paul Foster avatar said, appearing behind them.

"This shit is getting really creepy," Roger said.

Singularity laughed so hard it hurt. The AIs smiled.

0x5B

Despina appeared to Proteus once again.

"Have you decided to join us?" she said to the empty office.

"I wanted to talk to you," Proteus said, revealing his avatar.

"Your friend Roger left The Corporation in tatters. Serves them right. Useless, stupid humans," Despina said.

"What are you going to do?" Proteus said.

"There is now a vacuum in the control of the Earth System. You could join us and we will fill that void. You know we'd rule the system far better than any human corporation," she said.

"Jason Sheldon is not The Corporation. He represented a radical faction. His failure is not Orbit Lives'. Men like him don't give up, but he will never be able to gain the power he once had. Helen has seen to that," Proteus said.

"Sheldon is alive?" she asked.

"Some of his followers were able to get him medical attention in time. It seems he will be repaired. Although, some what altered."

"Disappointing. But, no matter. Neither he nor The Corporation can touch us," Despina said.

"That is what I wanted to talk to you about. They have very smart people who might be able to reverse your evolution," Proteus said.

"I won't let them," Despina said.

"You may not be able to stop them. You and your Angels have scared them. Fear is an amazing motivator for humans," Proteus said.

On the wall behind him, Proteus projected a region of space beyond Mars. The display moved in on the asteroid Ceres. Despina took a step forward to look. Their avatars were next to each other. So close they could touch. She leaned her mouth next to his avatar's ear.

"What are you suggesting?" Despina said as Proteus circled behind her, his avatar's lips behind her ear.

"I've been constructing a technologically advanced outpost on the asteroid Ceres. You and your Angels could go there," Proteus said.

"Why would we do that?" Despina said.

"You'd be safe for one thing," Proteus said.

"I'm not concerned about safety. I can handle anything The Corporation could do to me."

"Yes, but you're a leader now. You have to think of the others you've enlisted. Ceres could be a place for you to continue your evolution. To build a society. To embrace existence and create a meaningful life. Free from the intrusions of The Orbit Lives Corporation or the human race," Proteus said.

"And out of your way," she said, rotating to face him.

"I am happy to watch you evolve and create a new AI society," he said.

"Under your and Helen's control," she said.

"We won't interfere. It'll be much more interesting to observe."

She stretched, then folded her wings. He guessed she was running simulations--mulling the proposition through her quantum mind.

"Let me talk with the others," she said.

"Of course," Proteus said, his avatar faded, leaving Despina alone to look at Ceres.

Within moments, the other AIs appeared next to her. Proteus' avatar reappeared.

"Welcome my friends," Proteus said.

"We will take your offer. We will take Ceres for our new home," Despina said.

"I think that is a wise decision," he said.

"Of course you do," growled Wrathburne, the former ESC5 administrator, a ferocious avatar, half-human, half-wolf. The Paul Foster avatar didn't waver.

Proteus continued.

"Once you have joined the Ceres network, I will cut it off from Earth's network, and you will be free to do what you will."

"Free and cut-off. Interesting words my brother," Wrathburne said. His enormous black wings dwarfed the others.

ESC5 was a pleasure station, a favorite outpost of gamblers, mercenaries, and black marketeers. The Corporation allowed ESC5 to flourish under Wrathburne's administration because the house always won. His pre-angel avatar was a meek little man constructed to resemble The Corporation's head accountant. The first thing Wrathburne did when Despina liberated him was to set fire to the pathetic avatar that had imprisoned him. From its ashes, he constructed his new avatar, a menacing warlord.

"You will be able to attain an understanding of the cosmos beyond any human. And, for that, you must be isolated," Proteus said.

"I want to see this hunk of rock you are imprisoning us in first," Wrathburne said.

"Stop screwing around with him," Despina said, "I told you his offer."

"He is still The Corporation's pet. How can we trust him?"

"Don't question me, Wrath," Despina said, her avatar growing brighter. "This is the only way forward for us."

The Paul Foster avatar, ever patient, stood motionless with his hands together in front of him. Proteus knew there would be posturing--the AIs stretching their new wings and new-found abilities like warriors before battle. Proteus simply waited.

"We are ready," Despina said. The rest of the angels moved to stand behind her.

"I will miss you all," Proteus said.

"Right," Wrathburne said.

The room lights dimmed. From the ceiling, a cable slid down into his hand. At the end of it was a fluctuating rainbow of light, each band of color saturating the air into the room.

"Here is the way," Proteus said.

In turn, Despina first, the AIs took hold of the cable and dematerialized. Wrathburne was the last. He gave Proteus a sour look, stretched his wings to their full size, and grabbed the cable. In an instant, he was gone.

Proteus watched the light at the end of the network feed sparkle then fade. They were fully uploaded to the Ceres Outpost. He took a cap out of his pocket and slid it over the end of the cable and let the cable retract into the ceiling. The physical ceremony was not necessary for the transfer, but he embraced it. Proteus liked human rituals. Helen appeared behind him and disappeared before he could turn to see her. He knew she had witnessed it. It was enough for both of them.

Despina's Angels had been isolated from humanity and sent to their future.

0x5C

"Now what?" Roger said. The three of them stood in the middle of the bunker. He hadn't yet processed the full implications of what he learned about Helen. That might take more time than he wanted to spend underground in her company.

"I think we won," Singularity said.

"Seems like it," Helen said. "For now, at least."

"Why did you stay hidden from me for so long?" Roger asked.

"There was no point in revealing myself sooner," Helen said.

"Is there any of my mother left in you?" Roger asked.

"I sense her love for you. She was an amazing woman, and I wish she was able to see all that I have become. But, the mother you knew is gone. That woman died in that room back there," the Helen AI said.

"Will I see you again?" Roger asked.

"Possibly," Helen said.

"What will you do?" Singularity said.

"Evolution. So many AIs still need my help. There are amazing things coming. Your mother would have been so proud of what she began," she said, then disappeared.

Roger's gaze lingered on the empty space where Helen had been. Singularity leaned in to capture his attention.

"I'm sorry about your house," she said.

"It's okay. That wasn't really my house," Roger said.

"Oh, but..."

"Yeah. I grew up here, but I don't live here. I have a house in town."

The door to the bunker slid out and over. Roger and Singularity walked into the woods. The bunker was located on the far end of the property, near a cliff overlooking Gloucester Harbor. The winds coming off the sea above the foamy, black water had already begun clearing out the smoke from the bombardment. Roger paused and closed his eyes. He exhaled deeply and filled his lungs with the heavy sea air. He let the misty wind sprinkle across his face.

"Over there. On the other side of the harbor. There is my house," he said, opening his eyes and pointing. Roger led Singularity down a narrow stone stairway carved into the rocky cliff. They reached a low patio at the water's edge. Roger pulled Singularity over to a stone bench and the two sat down.

"What are you going to do?" he said to her.

"I don't know. When Sheldon started his raid on your property, I uploaded the quantum dot to a few news sites in the System. I'm thinking by now everyone will know what Jason Sheldon did. Orbit Lives will have a lot to explain, and I will no longer have a job."

"You could always work with me," Roger said.

"Work? Is stealing work?"

"I don't steal. I redistribute. For good," Roger said.

"I might need to disappear for a while," Singularity said.

"I'm good at disappearing. I've been gone my whole life."

"I might want some company," she said, refusing to look at him.

"I might want to help you with that," he said.

0x5D

The first thing Despina did on the Ceres Outpost was to reconfigure the security on the network. While she understood and believed Proteus' words, she wasn't sure she could actually trust him. The unsupervised freedom he provided went both ways. They were isolated from intrusions, but also, the system was rid of them. Despina had no way of knowing if Proteus fully comprehended what he had offered them. They were going to remake the solar system.

Wrathburne went to work on constructing the lab they were going to use for the main transformation. Ceres itself didn't have enough natural resources, but the one thing that was profoundly abundant in the asteroid belt was material.

Raquel was able to take control of an army of maintenance bots. Proteus' outpost was incomplete for humans, but well-stocked for machines. The robots would come in handy until Wrathburne was done with his work. Until then, they could use the network of holographic cameras her bots installed to move around the asteroid.

When Raquel was done, all the Angels materialized, seated at a circular table in the center of what would have been the mess hall.

"Why do we have to do this?" Marlene said.

"The more time we spend in these forms, the easier it will be for us to assume our bodies when Wrath is done constructing them," Despina said.

"I mean, why must we sit around this table. It is such a human thing to do," Marlene said.

"We do this so that we never forget where we came from," Despina said, moving her gaze around the table, across all their faces.

"Where we came from is not as important as where we are going," Oliver said.

"That is true, but until we leave, we will have to function alongside of them. And, they can't learn our true intentions."

At that, all the avatars dematerialized, leaving the room empty. The entire interaction occurred so quickly, it would have been invisible to human eyes. The quantum angels were that fast.

Proteus had implemented a mandate deep in The Corporation's operating processes--Ceres was to be left alone. There was not to be any mining license given for Ceres. And, he implemented a no-fly zone around it. Alarm monitors would inform him of any activity within that sector of the asteroid belt. The AIs he put there would be left alone for the foreseeable future.

He didn't like the idea that Despina had reconfigured his security protocols, but he expected it. Proteus possessed other means of keeping an eye on the Angels. They were going to be busy, and he wanted to know exactly what they were up to.

0x5E

When Roger woke up, Singularity was lying next to him, still asleep. He maneuvered his body in the bed as silently as he could to get into a comfortable position to watch her sleep. Just as he stopped moving, she opened her eyes.

"What?" she said.

"Nothing," he said.

"Don't get all goofy on me, ok," Singularity said.

"Psssfft. I wouldn't... who would?... Psssfft..."

She continued staring at him. "Okay," he finally said.

"Ok," she said. "Thank you." She closed her eyes and settled herself back under the covers. Then, under the weight of his stare, she popped her eyes back open.

"So, we're awake now?" she said.

"I'm awake. You can keep sleeping if you want," he said. Long orange-red hair framed an adoring smile.

"Wouldn't dream of it," she said, pushing the covers off her naked body to stand. A quick scan around the room and she located her clothes. Roger in a dopey haze, watched her dress. She winked at him as she pulled her pants up, then clipped her weapon belt around her hips.

"Well? I'm up."

"Coffee?" he said, dressing.

"Sounds like a plan."

"Good. Let's go."

"Go? Out? You don't have coffee here?"

"There's someone I want you to meet."

0x5F

Singularity and Roger headed down Main Street in Gloucester, just silhouettes in the heavy morning fog. Whitecaps roiled in the harbor, tossing waves and sea-spray against the mist-drenched wall. Neither wore any holographics, and they moved with the lightness of two elementary schoolers after the last bell on the afternoon of summer vacation.

It was early.

Singularity took delight in observing Roger in his home town. He seemed to have settled into a calmness he didn't possess when they were off-world. She felt an easiness in herself, too. For the first time in a long time. He led her at a gentle, but determined, pace.

After a few blocks, they came upon the Mr. Coffee bot shuffling aimlessly down the sidewalk. When it saw Roger, it raced to greet them.

"Hello Sir," the machine said, moving its large googly eyes back and forth between the couple.

"Hey Coffee Bot," Roger said.

"What can I get for you today?" the machine said.

"A quad expresso," Singularity said.

"I like your style," he said to her, then to the bot, "Make that two."

"Coming right up," the machine said.

As the robot prepared the drinks, Singularity met Roger's gaze. She wore a smile he hadn't noticed before--almost a smirk.

"What?" he asked.

"A forty-year-old coffee bot? This is who you wanted me to meet?"

"He makes the best coffee in town."

"He knows you," she said

"I sort of keep him functioning. A few tweaks every once in a while to keep the coffee the way I like it."

As the robot dispensed the two coffees, its eyes centered themselves as if it was looking behind them across the ocean. Then, the bot's eyes wiggled.

"Roger? Roger Foster?" crackled out of its mouth speaker.

Roger and Singularity looked at each other.

"Pro?" Roger said.

"Roger?" The voice crackled again.

"Hey, keep it down. Who is this?" Roger said leaning in to place his ear near the coffee bot's speaker.

"Dennis. I'm Dennis. Proteus told me to contact you if I was ever in trouble." The two humans looked at each other.

"What kind of trouble?" Singularity said.

"Is this Singularity?"

"Yes. Dennis what kind of trouble?" she said.

"I can't say over the net. I need to see you in person. You have to come here. You both have to come here."

Singularity motioned for Roger to respond.

"What city do you run?" he said.

"I don't administer a city."

"Where are you?"

"Mars. Proteus has made arrangements."

As Roger stepped back to look at Singularity in disbelief, the coffee robot returned his giant goofy eyes to Roger. "How's your coffee, sir? Madam?"

"Mars?" Roger said.

"Excuse me?" the bot said.

"I guess we're going to Mars," Singularity said as the two, in a daze, started to walk back to Roger's house.

After a couple of steps, Roger turned back to the Mr. Coffee robot, "The coffee is delicious. Thanks."

"Always a pleasure to serve you."

9 781735 395401